PRAISE FOR M. L. BUCHMAN

A fabulous soaring thriller.

— *TAKE OVER AT MIDNIGHT*, MIDWEST
BOOK REVIEW

Meticulously researched, hard-hitting, and suspenseful.

— *PURE HEAT*, PUBLISHERS WEEKLY,
STARRED REVIEW

Expert technical details abound, as do realistic military missions with superb imagery that will have readers feeling as if they are right there in the midst and on the edges of their seats.

— *LIGHT UP THE NIGHT*, RT REVIEWS, 4 1/2
STARS

Buchman has catapulted his way to the top tier of my favorite authors.

— FRESH FICTION

Nonstop action that will keep readers on the edge of their seats.

— TAKE OVER AT MIDNIGHT, LIBRARY JOURNAL

M L. Buchman's ability to keep the reader right in the middle of the action is amazing.

— LONG AND SHORT REVIEWS

The only thing you'll ask yourself is, "When does the next one come out?"

— WAIT UNTIL MIDNIGHT, RT REVIEWS, 4 STARS

The first...of (a) stellar, long-running (military) romantic suspense series.

— THE NIGHT IS MINE, BOOKLIST, "THE 20 BEST ROMANTIC SUSPENSE NOVELS: MODERN MASTERPIECES"

I knew the books would be good, but I didn't realize how good.

— NIGHT STALKERS SERIES, KIRKUS REVIEWS

Buchman mixes adrenalin-spiking battles and brusque military jargon with a sensitive approach.

— PUBLISHERS WEEKLY

13 times "Top Pick of the Month"

— NIGHT OWL REVIEWS

Tom Clancy fans open to a strong female lead will clamor for more.

— *DRONE*, PUBLISHERS WEEKLY

Superb! Miranda is utterly compelling!

— *BOOKLIST*, STARRED REVIEW

Miranda Chase continues to astound and charm.

— BARB M.

Escape Rating: A. Five Stars! OMG just start with *Drone* and be prepared for a fantastic binge-read!

— READING REALITY

The best military thriller I've read in a very long time. Love the female characters.

— *DRONE*, SHELDON MCARTHUR,
FOUNDER OF THE MYSTERY BOOKSTORE,
LA

THE COMPLETE SAILING STORIES

A SAILING ROMANCE STORY COLLECTION

M. L. BUCHMAN

SIGN UP FOR M. L. BUCHMAN'S NEWSLETTER TODAY

and receive:
Release News
Free Short Stories
a Free Book

Get your free book today. Do it now.
free-book.mlbuchman.com

Or join his Reader's Club:
https://rc.mlbuchman.com/join

CONTENTS

Other works by M. L. Buchman: *(* - also in audio)*

Action-Adventure Thrillers

Dead Chef
One Chef!
Two Chef!

Miranda Chase
*Drone**
*Thunderbolt**
*Condor**
*Ghostrider**
*Raider**
*Chinook**
*Havoc**
*White Top**
*Start the Chase**
*Lightning**
*Skibird**
*Nightwatch**

Science Fiction / Fantasy

Deities Anonymous
Cookbook from Hell: Reheated
Saviors 101

Contemporary Romance

Eagle Cove
Return to Eagle Cove
Recipe for Eagle Cove
Longing for Eagle Cove
Keepsake for Eagle Cove

Love Abroad
Heart of the Cotswolds: England
Path of Love: Cinque Terre, Italy

Where Dreams
Where Dreams are Born
Where Dreams Reside
*Where Dreams Are of Christmas**
Where Dreams Unfold
Where Dreams Are Written
Where Dreams Continue

Non-Fiction

Strategies for Success
Managing Your Inner Artist/Writer
*Estate Planning for Authors**
Character Voice
Narrate and Record Your Own
*Audiobook**

Short Story Series by M. L. Buchman:

Action-Adventure Thrillers

Dead Chef

Miranda Chase Origin Stories

Romantic Suspense

Antarctic Ice Fliers

US Coast Guard

Contemporary Romance

Eagle Cove

Other

Deities Anonymous (fantasy)

Single Titles

The Emily Beale Universe
(military romantic suspense)

The Night Stalkers
MAIN FLIGHT
The Night Is Mine
I Own the Dawn
Wait Until Dark
Take Over at Midnight
Light Up the Night
Bring On the Dusk
By Break of Day
Target of the Heart
Target Lock on Love
Target of Mine
Target of One's Own
NIGHT STALKERS HOLIDAYS
*Daniel's Christmas**
*Frank's Independence Day**
*Peter's Christmas**
Christmas at Steel Beach
*Zachary's Christmas**
*Roy's Independence Day**
*Damien's Christmas**
Christmas at Peleliu Cove

Henderson's Ranch
*Nathan's Big Sky**
*Big Sky, Loyal Heart**
*Big Sky Dog Whisperer**
*Tales of Henderson's Ranch**

Shadow Force: Psi
*At the Slightest Sound**
*At the Quietest Word**
*At the Merest Glance**
*At the Clearest Sensation**

White House Protection Force
*Off the Leash**
*On Your Mark**
*In the Weeds**

Firehawks
Pure Heat
Full Blaze
*Hot Point**
*Flash of Fire**
Wild Fire

SMOKEJUMPERS
*Wildfire at Dawn**
*Wildfire at Larch Creek**
*Wildfire on the Skagit**

Delta Force
*Target Engaged**
*Heart Strike**
*Wild Justice**
*Midnight Trust**

Emily Beale Universe Short Story Series

The Night Stalkers
The Night Stalkers Stories
The Night Stalkers CSAR
The Night Stalkers Wedding Stories
The Future Night Stalkers

Delta Force
Th Delta Force Shooters
The Delta Force Warriors

Firehawks
The Firehawks Lookouts
The Firehawks Hotshots
The Firebirds

White House Protection Force
Stories

Future Night Stalkers
Stories (Science Fiction)

ABOUT THIS BOOK

Five tales of romance and boats collected together on a voyage of love, travel, and adventure in a world afloat.

- *Solo Crossing* - sailing away from it all can chart a fresh course through the past
- *Return Passage* - setting a course for home leads to a new future
- *Narrowboat Goddess* - love on the English canals
- *Carved from Sand* - when sand sculpture and sailboat racing collide
- *Santa and the Pirate Queen* - true love at Christmas only needs a pirate ship

Pull on your sou'wester and snuggle down for a good ride.

SOLO CROSSING

ABOUT THIS STORY

When a man loses everything,
that is when the possibilities begin.

Ron had it all: the career, the big house, the sailing hobby, the great girlfriend. He always looked ahead, never behind. Never had to. Until the day it all went away.

Left with nothing but his boat and a childhood dream of circumnavigating the globe, he set sail, looking for the future.

When a storm lashes him during his first crossing, he finally looks at what he left behind.

1

Strain of Juan de Luca
Washington State
1/2 kilometer offshore

The temperature dropped a few degrees as Ron's sailboat broke free of the Strait and rode out onto the broad Pacific Ocean off the Washington coast. The slight change to the sky-blue, sun-warmed May day shouldn't have sent a shiver across his shoulders, but it took an act of will to stop it.

For better or worse he'd done it, and felt as if he'd shed a hundred pounds.

That was a good sign, right?

Actually, a lot more weight than that. Someone had once told him that the tidal flow through the Strait of Juan de Fuca was four billion gallons. Every twelve hours, sixteen cubic kilometers of seawater rushed in and back out along its hundred-and-sixty-kilometer length. Around the thousand inlets and islands of Puget Sound and the inside passage of Vancouver Island, the tide rose and fell three meters twice a day. And now that massive flow had flushed his sailboat out into the Pacific Ocean like a piece of flotsam.

No, thoughtlessly aiming ahead was his past. *Climb the corporate ladder. Buy a nicer house. Drive a better car. Work waaaay too many hours.* Starting today, rather than passively riding the tides of his own life, he could make choices.

He'd dug his own burnout hole fair and square. Worse, he'd spent over a decade turning that rut into a mine-deep trench. It was only now that he was starting to see its vast, dark depths.

A rut with a view. Hell of an upgrade, Ron.

For the first time, maybe ever, he saw the cascading pile-up of his life to date. Like a whole chain of cars on a foggy interstate. And it had all been his own doing. To himself.

It was a struggle, but Ron managed not to puke over the side of the boat. Once he suppressed that urge as well, he repointed the boat to stop the flapping of the sails.

This was a new chapter...or "the last act of a desperate man." He really didn't need Sheriff Bart from *Blazing Saddles* pointing out the possibility that this was the most colossal mistake he'd ever made, which would be saying something.

The whole crowd of gulls that had been screaming overhead, asking if he was a fishing boat, ceased their constant inquiries and settled onto the waves or flew back to shore. One by one they fell behind until only the occasional bird swooped down to see if he was interesting before continuing on its way.

Nothing at all like a fishing boat, his forty-eight-foot Cheoy Lee was a sailboat designed for an ocean crossing. She was fiberglass white with mahogany trim and handrails. Clean lines, cutter rigged with a single tall mast, and he especially liked the mid-ship's cockpit tucked under the main boom. Rather than low in the stern, the ship's wheel and U-shaped teak bench seat perched a third of the way forward. He had a cloth dodger with plastic windows when he needed sun protection in the tropics, but here in the mild Pacific Northwest, he liked being open to the wind and occasional bits of spray.

Ron eyed the land to the north and south warily in case it was some kind of trick and those sixteen cubic kilometers were about to suck him back into his old life. The strait was twenty kilometers wide here, from the southern curve of Vancouver Island, a dark green line to the north, to Cape Flattery, close aboard to the south. More importantly to the Cape Flattery lighthouse on Tatoosh Island.

He'd always thought that Tatoosh looked like an upside-down saucepan half-sunk in the ocean when he'd viewed it from land. The circular island lay a kilometer offshore the northwesternmost point of the continental US. Its ten-story-tall vertical cliffs and flat top three hundred meters across was only broken by the old lighthouse and a handful of trees hardy enough to claw upward despite the horrendous storms that so often battered this section of the coast.

Open water lay to his right and Tatoosh had definitely fallen several degrees behind the port beam of the *Brise*. He was definitely at sea.

He'd wanted to name his Cheoy Lee 48 *Mu*—after H. P. Lovecraft's lost continent. Teresa had pointed out that naming a sailboat after a mythical land was one thing. But naming it after a mythical land that had sunk forever beneath the ocean after a war with Atlantis might not be the best idea.

He didn't speak French, but she did, and she'd made *Breeze* sound so lovely in that language that he'd caved easily. She'd always been able to do that to him since the first time she'd asked him out for pizza.

Ron stared upward at his sails, blinding in the sunny morning sun despite his sunglasses, and drawing well with the northwesterlies as he turned downwind. Then he looked out at the long eight-foot rollers driving landward. Last landfall for these waves had probably been the Aleutian Islands or Japan at twice the distance. Maybe even New Zealand at twice that again.

He drew in a deep breath of air so fresh it might have been newly created for his use alone. The cleansing flow almost tickled as it dragged the crap out of his lungs.

The corporate crap.

The house renovation crap that had taken up every spare moment and dollar when he wasn't scrambling to keep a computer network functional on an office-wide scale.

The whole social scene crap that he'd always sucked at, and felt incompetent about every time he was somehow snared in by his friends. At least the few friends who hadn't shed him as too much bother long ago.

He nudged the wheel over a few points and eased the sails to match the new heading. His first planned landfall would be in San Francisco for his deep-sea adventure. There were sea stacks to well off the coast, but fifty kilometers offshore would leave him plenty of leeway and still place him within ten hours of reaching port in a storm. Less if he used the engine.

The only other time he'd been out on the open ocean he'd been nine years old with Dad. The feeling of freedom had been terribly exhilarating and remarkably brief.

Every summer since before he could remember, the family had spent two weeks in a small cottage on the Cape Cod shore with other friends in nearby rentals. It was the big annual outing for the family and for their fourteen-foot Sunfish sailboat. One family had a ski boat, another a small dinghy with an outboard good for puttering out to the best mid-harbor sandbars for digging clams. The Sunfish was a sprightly sailer that Ron had mastered by the time he was seven, at least on calm waters.

One bright day, he and Dad had taken the Sunfish through the cut that separated Nauset Harbor, with plenty of good sailing for such a small boat, out onto the Atlantic.

Ron twisted to look behind him as if he could see across the continent to that long-ago adventure. *Three thousand miles and twenty years away, dude.*

They hadn't made it more than a hundred yards offshore. A big wave had capsized them mere minutes from shore. They'd had lifejackets, and it was a common occurrence in the tiny boat and easily rectified under normal conditions. If there hadn't been a handy sandbar to duck behind, it would have been much harder to right the boat in the big rollers sweeping toward the beach.

Ron laughed, though it was a sad sound that caught hard in his throat.

Back then his father had known *everything*. He was Dad after all. In retrospect, Ron could see that the big wave that had flipped them into the ocean had probably been because his father had sailed them too close to that sandbar to begin with. The rise in the ocean bed had created the big wave and the capsize had been inevitable.

And now, in his thirties, Ron knew he was a far better sailor than Dad had ever been despite all of Dad's snide comments to the contrary.

The little Sunfish sailboat had taught Ron to dream long before that brief sea adventure. A dream of circumnavigating the globe. As a pre-teen, he'd read every book he could find at the library from Cook and Bligh to

Chichester and Slocum. But he wasn't supposed to be doing this first big crossing solo.

He and Pop Sam, sailing together around the world. That had been his childhood fantasy. But Pop Sam had died the year when Ron was eight, a year before even that first adventure out onto a big ocean.

Not once had he ever thought of going with his father, and in retrospect, he could finally guess why. With Dad everything was a competition and always had been. Yet sailing, whether alone in Nauset Harbor on Cape Cod or during a blustery race on Puget Sound with a crew of eight, was the one place that Ron ever felt as if everything was easy.

Yeah, a whole lot of shit he was leaving behind. And, God damn it, he was going to leave it behind *now*.

He spun the wheel to starboard then winched in the main and jib sails as he turned to head farther offshore.

Not San Francisco. He'd already been there a few times anyway. If he was going around the world then, by God, he was going around the world. He could always visit San Francisco on the way home if he still wanted to.

New life! New course! Hoo-rah! Or did military guys say *Oo-rah? Or... Doesn't matter. Sail on!* Yeah, he'd use that.

New life! New course! Sail on! It was good. And change from his trench-deep rut was way past due.

He'd cross the California current as he rode it south to well offshore Baja, then pick up the high side of the northern equatorial current to the west.

As if confirming the rightness of his choice, a pair of dolphins slid in front of him, coming from somewhere dolphiny. Or porpoisy.

Then the Mock turtle said, 'No wise fish would go anywhere with a porpoise.'

Thank you Alice in Wonderland.

Though maybe he was going to sea with a sense of *dolphin*. If so, what did that mean? He really had to look up how to tell them apart.

As *Brise* forged ahead, the pair played in the bow waves, rarely jumping clear of the water, but enjoying the race.

Ron trimmed for a little more speed, not that he could begin to match them, but it was fun to make it more interesting for them. For fifteen minutes they cruised along with him before disappearing as abruptly as they'd arrived. Did dolphins, or porpoises, have underwater teleportation? Sonar that created a large blinking, *Fun over there!* sign in their heads? That would be cool.

Brise journeyed on without dolphins or sea gulls to keep her company. She rode well over the waves. The Cheoy Lee was a perfect compromise between a lean uncomfortable racing boat and a slow, fat and wallowing cruiser. Big enough to be comfortable as a liveaboard and narrow enough to move well. The only sounds were the slight slap of the rigging as he crested each wave, the continuous background rush of water peeled open by his fin keel, and the shushing of the ocean closing behind him, leaving no more than a whitish patch of water, full of turbulated air that dissipated quickly.

With all the lines routed into the cockpit, she was easy to single-hand. No crew required, just he and *Brise.* It was enough.

Next stop Hawaii. His wide swing to the south, rather than striking for the most direct line across the easter gyre of the North Pacific, should provide much steadier winds.

Maybe he'd find a worthy sailing companion there.

It certainly hadn't been Teresa Compton.

2

Heceta Bank
Oregon Coast
87 km offshore

Ron stuffed in his earplugs and yanked up his hood before clawing his way up onto deck. The moment he opened the hatch, the rain drummed against his rain slicks.

It had been maddeningly loud until he'd located where he'd stowed the earplugs—squished up bits of toilet paper hadn't cut it. At least it was a cool rain so that he wouldn't sweat to death under the slicks. He did end up being clammy all day, with cold little rivulets finding the odd gap to soak his clothes in scattered, annoying ways.

Up on deck, he snapped his safety harness onto the jack line first and closed the hatch behind him second. The line ran bow-to-stern along the deck. If he fell, the short line would keep him aboard the boat, or at least attached to it.

It wasn't really called for in this weather as the seas weren't particularly rough—as if the rain was beating it flat. But he was already staggeringly tired and he didn't trust himself not to stumble overboard. The boat was heeled fifteen degrees and the lifelines that ran around the entire perimeter of the deck were only thigh high. He couldn't escape the image of sliding down the deck and having the lifeline toss him in a head-over-heels somersault into the waves rushing by so close.

Brise's autopilot would keep heading the boat south-southwest leaving him behind to drown on his own.

To sleep. Perchance to dream. Hamlet, buddy, you had it easy. At least you were on dry land.

The Cheoy Lee handled well but he was not adapted to sleeping while rolling side-to-side as they climbed and descended the rollers at an angle. And with each roll, every line slapped or twanged or twinged or found another new sound to make. Slapping sounds were the domain of the waves against the fiberglass hull. With each crested wave, the mast swung left then right, then left again, snapping the sail loudly as it refilled to draw ahead.

He also hadn't slept well because of general paranoia. He knew that would ease with time, but last night he'd stuck his head up through the hatch every thirty minutes, sometimes every twenty, to inspect that everything was as it should be. He was running across the massively busy shipping lanes of the US West Coast and it was all too easy to imagine being run down.

Ron blinked up into the rain as he settled by the wheel in the cockpit. It was hard to believe that the little foot-across ball of the aluminum radar reflector near the mast top was brighter on a ship's radar than the rest of his boat combined. Wet cloth sails returned notoriously little signal and the rounded aluminum mast scattered rather than reflected any radar sweep from another ship.

That was assuming that any approaching ship had a crew that was actually paying attention.

There was a horror story common enough for him to believe it had happened. It was of a ship coming into port, only to have a dockhand point in surprise at the mast and sails snagged on the anchor with no sailboat attached. Even when he'd managed to wedge himself where the berth's mattress met the hull to stop his rolling about, that fear—but one of many—had kept him awake.

The guard zone setting on Ron's marine radar should do the job of waking him if there were problems, like an approaching ship. But experience hadn't yet built trust in that either. Sure, it had worked fine in Puget Sound, but what about out here on the ocean. His brain knew it was fine, but his nervous system was twitchier than a rebooting server with configuration issues. Maybe, if he mounted a second small wind turbine in the rigging to doubly ensure that the batteries stayed charged to run the equipment, his nerves would chill. Probably not.

On deck and conscious not by choice, he did his morning routine.

Only Day Three since driving past Tatoosh Island and already he had a routine. That had to be another good sign.

Embrace routine. Because you're sure too tired to actually think. A good maxim that he should write down somewhere...somewhere that wasn't soaked to the skin by the unending rain drilling against his slicks and pounding on the deck. *A bright cheerful patter on a tin roof? Not!*

He walked up the length of the deck, checking each line and fitting as he went. The jack line had been run down the port side, so he trailed his harness clip along behind him which banged and clattered over every fitting and winch. He was too unstable on his feet to keep it lifted off the deck.

For the return, he hadn't rigged a line down the starboard side. Ducking back and forth under the sails, around the dinghy tied upside down to the deck, and offering a brief prayer to the white canister of the life raft that he'd never need it, had been arduous enough the first two days. But he didn't have the energy to rig a second jack line today as he'd meant to yesterday.

"Fine. It all looks good from here." His voice was the first sound he'd heard not made by the boat or the ocean since he'd left behind the gulls off the Strait of Juan de Fuca.

He sounded like a dying frog.

"You're all alone. It's okay to talk to yourself." Not much better. And was that true? Or was he losing it?

He liked music, but he'd been told so often that he sang flat that he'd given up singing along to anything, even in the car. The thought of going below to plug in something on the stereo had him staring aloft at the wind generator again. Six little blades in a three-foot housing—it was *supposed* to produce plenty of power. But he needed the energy for nav and radio gear. He didn't *need* the music.

Ron stayed on deck.

"So where are we?" As if he didn't already know. Nope! The sound of his voice was too sad all alone on the ocean. Maybe he'd keep his thoughts to himself just as *Brise* kept her thoughts to herself.

He looked east. The sheeting rain limited visibility to perhaps a kilometer. Sitting once more in the cockpit, the horizon was only five kilometers anyway. And the nearest land was a hundred.

Even though he'd sprung for the unit that could read down to seven hundred meters, the depth sounder said the bottom was beyond range. He shut it off to save power.

Brise was out over the great deep and the abyssal plain

lay three kilometers below. Even the great Heceta Bank section of the continental shelf lay well to the east of him.

And beyond the Heceta Bank lay Heceta Head and the Heceta Lighthouse Bed and Breakfast.

It had been his and Teresa's first vacation together. They'd been dating for six months and she'd wanted to drive down the Oregon Coast. A fan of her mystery novels had gifted her a night in the B&B, which was their southernmost stop. They'd wandered down the coast for three days, following Highway 101's lazy meanderings through quaint towns and tacky tourist enclaves that still smelled of the sea and endured the battering of the raw Pacific Ocean.

They'd strolled through the surprisingly interesting Columbia River Maritime Museum, eaten fish and chips at Mo's in Lincoln City like any good tourist, and been skunked on a whale sightseeing day out of the "World's Smallest Harbor" in Depoe Bay. It had been such a lovely day that they hadn't cared about the lack of whales. Their relationship had still been in that early phase where they couldn't be in close enough contact.

Together they'd gazed out at the deep ocean to where he sailed even now. That's when he'd told her of his silly childhood dream of sailing around the world with his grandfather. Teresa had done as she always did whenever he had an idea: *You should do it!*

As if it was so easy.

He'd been starting a new corporate job the day they returned from their drive. A promotion to head a key department after a series of unrelated turnovers had coincided to gut the group. They'd tasked him with keeping it afloat and improving the overall operation while he was at it. It was the biggest project he'd ever tackled and the first time he'd done one for a national-level corporation. There was room to climb here in ways that none of his past positions at smaller firms had offered.

She'd kept after him for the rest of the trip. In her gentle way, of course: cheerful, easy-going...and tenacious as hell.

So what would be your first port of call?

When they'd stopped at Newport's harbor, she'd insisted that they stroll along the waterfront.

Could any of these boats in the marina cross the ocean?

He had done a fair amount of sailing, moments stolen from work over the years. Occasionally running in races up and down Puget Sound. He'd risen to the point that it wasn't unusual for a skipper to call him in to helm the boat for a race that the skipper himself couldn't attend. His favorite had been a Swan 60 cruiser/racer that had handled like a dream. They weren't major races, first prize was often little more than bragging rights, and he'd earned that several times.

Teresa had even hauled him into a brokerage. She knew nothing about boats. They'd spent hours, with her charming both himself and broker, touring the different types of boats as an *education for her.*

She had made it seem like a game, a bit of whimsical fun to enliven their trip. But the idea had begun to take form in the back of his mind as perhaps more than a childhood dream. Somehow he'd never connected the idea of getting on a boat whenever he could break away from work, with that long-lost idea.

At Heceta Head, they'd toured the old lighthouse and relaxed to watch the sunset from the wide front porch of the keeper's cottage turned B&B. The air had smelled as fresh there as it ever had in his life. Teresa curled up beside him under a throw blanket in an Adirondack chair meant for one. The dream seemed impossibly possible there.

Ron had known it wouldn't happen, but it wasn't a bad dream.

They'd made love in a small room facing the ocean and lit by the moonlight. A thin fog had slid in toward midnight. That, in turn, had revealed the lighthouse beam sweeping toward the great unknown, beckoning them to watch it through the night.

The gourmet seven-course breakfast, one of the B&B's trademarks, had completed the perfect night.

Teresa had grabbed a brochure of the Oregon lighthouses from the front table. They'd planned to drive back to Seattle up through the Willamette Valley, maybe even visit the wine country though neither of them knew much about it. Instead they'd returned up the coast visiting every lighthouse and scenic overlook that they'd missed on the way south.

All that seemed impossibly far away—lost in the foggy past of a year ago.

The unending drum of rain is your life now.

It already felt as if it would never end, drumming on his slicks. The fat, wind-driven drops hit hard enough to sting through the thick rubberized whatever this was. And still he was nodding in and out of a doze on the cockpit seat.

Had they been in love then?

Ron tried to remember when the *love* part of their relationship had begun but couldn't pin it down. It had been real. He remembered that much.

He strongly suspected that it had started somewhere between when she had begun to dream his dream for him, and when he'd finally begun to dream it for himself.

3

San Francisco Bay
California
169 km due west

Stupid cliches and stereotypes! They'd always bugged Ron.

But California was being true to both.

The Pineapple Express, the warm winds driving from Hawaii toward the Oregon and Washington Coast—and dumping eighty-three kajillion gallons of water on his head in seven straight days—had ceased sometime in the night. He'd drawn even with San Francisco, and Mother Nature had shut off the faucet with one sharp twist of her almighty hand.

Seven days, which should have taken him five, spent battering into a head wind that had forced him to either tack much farther offshore than he wanted to go, or sent him racing toward land he didn't want to reach. But the due-south course he wanted had put him in a very uncomfortable broadside to the Express' waves. Instead he'd done the exhausting work of tacking back and forth to take the waves on one quarter or the other.

But as he sailed opposite central California, the rain had disappeared. The winds had curled in behind him until they were smooth northerlies. The silence as he spread the sails to dead downwind was almost haunting—no whistling wind in the rigging, no pounding rain, no hard slap of wave or sail.

Brise rushed effortlessly ahead.

He now cruised at nearly the same speed as the low rollers. Rather than being slammed every ten or fifteen seconds, the long swells caught up with him every few minutes, gently lifting the stern of the *Brise,* sweeping smoothly underneath, and then setting the bow down like a giant rocking chair.

And, to complete the cliché, the sun now glittered off the bluest rolling ocean. The last of the storm clouds lingered far to the north as no more than a low fog soon forgotten. The more distance the better.

For twelve hundred kilometers, he'd managed not to turn back. Not to give in to the urge to turn for port, sell the damned boat, and fly home.

But then he'd be yet another person who had dared to dream—and failed.

"I tried, but it was too much bother." The perfect sunny day scoffed at him when he tried out different versions aloud. "It was so much harder than I expected." No one had promised him it would be easy.

Nothing had been easy in his life. Except maybe Teresa. Maybe that had been the final problem.

He remembered talking with his boss at a law firm where Ron had run the IT for a major case, tracking and coding five million pages of project documents spread across five states and three continents. Fred had all the trappings of success: a founder and named partner of one of Seattle's Top Ten law firms, the fancy house, still married to his college girlfriend, kids all successfully launched, and he was about to retire to luxury.

Got out of school and decided that life sucked. So, I did what I was supposed to do but can't say as I ever enjoyed it much.

When Ron had mentioned the conversation to Dad, he'd shrugged a maybe. Just what Ron had always wanted to be, a key player in his father's disappointing life. He certainly wasn't going to do that with his own.

Sure he was a nerd and a geek. But unlike his engineer father who was only good with machines, Ron had struggled for more. He'd learned how to be good with people, or at least better than the average computer nerd. It had made him a project manager with a tech twist. He'd escaped the programmer trap of being an asocial cog in someone else's project.

The problem had been that all of the learning and growth, all that internal work, had made it so that he didn't fit in at either end of the spectrum: the extrovert power players or the asocial geeks. Instead he'd discovered a no-man's land in between.

Shake it off! The past was clinging like barnacles on the hull and that would never do.

Action! Do something! Move about! More good maxims.

He began the cleanup of the boat that he'd avoided during the seven days of battering rain. There was a squeak in the boom vang's upper pulley that sang with every tiny shift of the mainsail. On a frayed end on a backstay adjuster line, he snipped off the end and pulled out his splicing tools to create a clean butt end that wouldn't unravel again. He made the rounds with a big screwdriver to make sure that all of the tracks were well snugged down.

Without really being conscious he was doing it, he had begun looking for a sailboat six months after that trip to Heceta Head with Teresa.

He'd asked a skipper of a Valiant 40 if he wanted a hand for a Saturday sail so that he could see how that particular boat handled.

An old guy ran an older fifty-six-foot wooden bugeye ketch as a dinner-cruise sailboat. He'd treated Teresa to an evening sail but spent most of his time chatting with the skipper about cruising. Tony had spent years crossing from Puget Sound in the summer to Corpus Christi, Texas in the winters. Twice each year through the Panama Canal —singlehanded.

Ron had started focusing on sailing solo after that. Sometimes he'd borrow a boat. Other times, he'd go out with a like-minded sailor, but with only one of them managing the whole boat at a time.

Sail *with* someone?

Since the dream of sailing with Pop Sam had died with his grandfather, he'd always sort of assumed he'd sail alone.

But now Teresa was in his life. Would she want to go offshore with him? He almost asked her a hundred different times, but always found a reason not to. When they celebrated their one-year dating anniversary, it had been the longest he'd ever been with anyone. He didn't want to mess that up.

Six months after that...

Yeah. Six months after that, the real opportunity had come up. Everything had seemed to happen at once.

So damned fast. He looked up at the sky. *Universe, were*

you kicking my butt? It was something Teresa often talked about.

When everything is moving a little to fast, you're in the flow of right action.

Like the universe knows more about what's good for me than I do? he'd asked.

She nodded an *of course* in that way of hers.

What had happened was a buddy on the sailor circuit knew someone selling a Cheoy Lee 48. Designed by Bob Perry in 1980 as an offshore racing/cruiser. The owner had run it in the Vic-Maui race a few times, but wanted a smaller boat, a daysailer to bob about on Lake Washington now that he had a family.

Teresa had been deep in drafting a fresh murder plot for her next book. When she was like that, she couldn't be distracted by anything, except Chinese takeout. In the end run of a novel, even that didn't do it. He'd learned that he was on his own at such times.

She'd sailed with him as often as not and had quickly learned to be a capable deckhand. But while going offshore wasn't her passion, it had slowly become his.

He'd taken the Cheoy Lee 48 out once with the owner and knew he'd found his boat. As soon as the marine surveyor had signed off on its soundness, he'd written the check. It would mean selling his house and moving aboard. Funny. He hadn't even thought about that until the deal was done.

Once he had? A space that fit him instead of the bigger-house-is-better image he'd inherited from Dad. He sold the house fully furnished. No yard maintenance! *Oh yeah! House maintenance traded for boat maintenance? Any damn day of the week.*

Ron knelt on the deck and scrubbed cleanser across the

fiberglass decking. The clip on his safety harness had left marks on the white surface as he'd dragged it up and down the jack line for the entire last week.

The autopilot was holding him steady on the wind.

He no longer had to remember to look up for passing ships that might cause him trouble. Every minute or so, he did a quick scan around automatically, barely noticing the break in his rhythm.

Proactive. Efficiency. He was rocking this new life.

San Francisco was one of the busiest ports on the West Coast and the clutter of sea traffic reflected that. But the Seattle / Tacoma Port Alliance was bigger and in much more confined waters. Out here on the open ocean, the clutter of ships was actually spread quite far apart.

Also, the radar had beeped its alarm enough times now for him to trust its judgement.

Early on, Ron had second-guessed the impulse purchase of *Brise* a thousand times. But now that he was sailing smoothly beneath the shining Californian sunshine, he could feel that weight sloughing off as well.

By the time Teresa had emerged from her writing, he'd already moved what he was keeping onto the boat and had his house up for sale. He'd showed *Brise* to her without explaining that he'd bought it already.

The moment she figured that out, she'd thrown her arms around him and wept. Not little happy tears, but great heaving sobs that had alarmed other liveaboards along the dock. Heads had popped out of hatches to make sure everything was okay, but he hadn't known how to tell.

Clueless as usual! He'd held her, unsure what else to do.

I was so afraid you'd let your dream die, she'd finally managed. *That would have been so tragic. I'd thought I'd lost you to your job.*

But he still had his job—or had at that time.

And like the idiot he was, he'd looked from her tear-stained face to the boat and back to her.

His dream?

It had merely been the next thing he'd wanted to do. He'd never quite connected it to his dream possibly coming true. The idea that he might actually chuck it all and go sailing around the world had been...surprising.

Surprising and unlikely as hell! That's what he'd though in that moment as she clung to him at the dockside.

But against all odds and doubts, it *had* come true.

He was living the dream now, wasn't he? How weird was that?

He made himself a tuna sandwich from the last of his bread, fished a couple of carrots and a can of Coke out of the refrigerator, and took it up to the cockpit. It was his first meal, more involved than an energy bar, that he'd eaten on deck since he'd left Port Townsend.

Ron leaned back in the sun. He checked the horizon, his heading, and the set of the sails in a single glance.

It was just him and *Brise* but they were on their way.

Alone.

The tuna sandwich tasted like cardboard.

4

Central Baja California
Mexico
1,193 km due west

The sun lasted for four glorious days...

Then the storm caught up with the *Brise.* It was noon but it looked like the middle of the night.

Ron had seen it coming in several ways.

He'd spotted the first of it as high cirrus clouds, horse tails, off northern Baja.

The weather in Seattle had been very predictable because almost all of it came in off the Pacific without being stirred around by passing over whole sections of the continent. The high wisps typically preceded a still-high gray haze that let through most of the sunlight but blocked the blue sky. Depending on how fast the transition was, it could then be anywhere from one to three days for the heavy overcast and rain to move in.

This was coming from a different direction, but he

wondered if it would follow the same pattern. He didn't have to wonder for long.

He was off central Baja by the time the NOAA Weatherfax forecast over his long-range radio had looked worrisome. An early-season storm had been born over the heated waters of the Sea of Cortez, trapped between Baja and mainland Mexico. It had escaped into the Pacific and built rapidly over the warming north equatorial current he'd been hoping to ride west to Hawaii.

The weather radar began painting disconcerting bands of green, then yellow, and finally red.

The storm was between him and the land, so he couldn't turn east to make a run for a port, any port. Besides, with his distance offshore, it would be a three-day run, probably four or five against the prevailing winds. Any hopes of driving clear to the north or south were dashed by the storm's rapid growth. It soon spanned six hundred kilometers and he was near enough the center that he wasn't getting out of its way.

Then NOAA predicted that somewhere past his position it would shift from whole gale to the first hurricane of the season on its way to beat on Hawaii. For now it was only a Force 10 storm—only. The same strength that had devastated the Fastnet race around the UK four decades before. He'd read Rousmaniere's book, *Fastnet, Force 10*. Fifteen died, dozens of boats were abandoned, and several sank. Over a hundred were rescued by lifeboat services and helicopters.

Panic doesn't solve shit! He'd learned that when dealing with a crashed computer network or a boss who'd tipped off the deep end of rage about something.

But damn! Panic sure felt tempting, didn't it?

The biggest storm he'd ever sailed in had been thirty-five knots, forty miles an hour, in the San Juan Islands of

Puget Sound. He'd watched twenty-five-foot boats getting slapped about by the story-tall waves. Luckily, he'd been aboard a fifty-foot full-keel ketch that day and she'd ridden such weather easily.

In a Force 10 storm out here on the Pacific, he'd be facing fifty-to-sixty knot winds and seas that were—he looked at the storm force table in two different references before he could quite believe it—ten- to fifteen-meter waves. He tried to imagine waves three to five stories tall and all it did was make his head hurt. The very top of his mast was only six stories tall.

Way too real!

Ignore that shit!

Go! Go! Go! Like one of those SWAT team moments in a movie. *SWAT team of one. Here I come!*

First, Ron made sure everything was well stowed and that the hatches were all battened down. He prepared two days of meals that he could simply grab and eat cold if necessary. Cooking on his small propane stove would be out of the question despite the gimble that would let it swing to stay level as the boat rocked side-to-side. If he encountered end-to-end pitching, it definitely wouldn't work.

He'd only had to reef a sail a few times in his life, so he did it well before the heavy winds hit. He lowered the main a third of the way, then went down the sail running a tie that went through each of the grommets in the middle of the sail and cinching it around the main boom. The remaining one-third of his main looked ridiculous in the fine sailing wind he presently had, but he'd rather lose sailing time and be ready.

He left the big genoa sail drawing at the headstay that went from the tip of the bow to the top of the mast. It had roller furling, so he wouldn't even need to leave the cockpit later to roll it up around that front wire. Then he could pull out the storm jib from the fore stay that started several feet aft of the bow and attached two-thirds of the way up the mast. It was a much smaller sail so he could still have enough way on, enough speed to control the boat even in a high wind.

Hopefully.

Just in case, he spent a while studying the storm anchor. It didn't sound scary, it sounded terrifying. If the storm grew to be too awful, but before it became *too* awful, he'd have to douse sails and set the sea anchor. It was an underwater parachute twelve feet in diameter and eighteen feet long. It would drag in the sea at the end of five hundred feet of line, literally an anchor in the water. The wind and waves would drag *Brise* downwind against that line and hold her bow on into the maelstrom.

What else? What else?

Prep the crew? Just me. Done!

Set the frequency to call a May Day if everything went all Fastnet, Force 10 on him. Already done. Right. Standard practice: to always be set to the emergency frequency so that he could hear others in trouble. Done!

Crap!

Out of ideas, there was nothing to do now but worry and wait.

Six hours later, the leading edge was on him. It hadn't eased in, it had slammed. The sea rose before a wind that no longer washed over *Brise*. Instead it made the rigging hum, and then begin to whistle as it lashed the building waves ever higher.

Act early! Right!

Ron hauled the main boom tightly amidships and rolled up the storm jib. The double-reefed main sail, and hadn't putting in the second reef been a huge pain to do, kept him roughly pointed into the wind.

He fought his way out of the marginal safety of the cockpit. On hands and knees he crawled forward, with the jack line hooked to his safety harness as a guide.

Each wave slammed in from a different direction. He should have...what? Had another person on board?

Duh!

A wave, strangely warm here near the equator after years sailing in the frigid waters of Puget Sound, slammed him into the low side of the cabin. Its retreat tried to drag him through the lifelines. The next washed him aft along the deck. He could feel the heat from clutching the jack line that would have been rope burn if he hadn't pulled on fingerless bicycle gloves.

Good decision.

When he could breathe again, Ron was amazed that his autoinflate life vest hadn't decided he was underwater and triggered.

He finished the crawl forward to double-check that the line for the sea anchor was secure before he deployed it over the side. Just as he decided it was, the bow drove deep into a wave, green water slamming aboard and driving the bow even deeper into the water. He managed a half breath, thick with salt spray, and held it as he was submerged.

This time his life jacket decided he was in trouble and inflated with a hard snap against his chest.

The float pushed him to the surface at the same moment that the wave drained overboard. Instead of slamming down onto the deck, the life preserver cushioned the impact.

That's something at least.

Coughing and half gagging for breath, Ron rode the next wave back along the deck. He was almost washed past the cockpit and dumped into the stern lifelines before he could stop himself. He flopped into the cockpit and lay on one of the benches like a beached fish, until the next wave came at him sideways, high enough to reach the cockpit as he rode broadside into it.

Struggling to sit up, he tossed over the trip line so that he could recover the sea anchor later, then the sea anchor itself. He briefly snubbed the line. With a sharp jerk, the pressure on the line increased a hundred-fold and he let it run. The brief snub of the line had fully deployed the sea anchor, hopefully, and it was now an underwater parachute instead of a useless snarl of cloth.

Less than a minute later, a low thrum sounded through the boat, a deep vibration he could feel through his butt on the cockpit seat despite the pounding of the storm. The sea anchor had reached the end of its heavy rode, made of five hundred feet of three-quarter-inch nylon line and thirty feet of chain.

The bow swung into the wind and waves, and the boat settled down almost immediately. With a couple of bungie cords he lashed the steering wheel to center the rudder, decided that *Brise* was riding well with the double-reefed main, and collapsed once more onto the cockpit's bench seat.

Did it. Without dying! Whoot!

The storm continued to howl. The wind-lashed salt spray was warm against his face as it tugged against his inflated life vest. He'd have to deal with that before he crawled forward in half an hour to make sure the sea anchor's line wasn't chafing. For now, he wasn't moving an inch.

Thousands of sailors had ridden out hundreds of storms safely enough. He could do that. The motion wasn't smooth in the storm, but he could feel the solid hold of the sea anchor keeping him safe.

Stay calm. Stay focused. Those were the keys.

Slowly he turned his attention to the world around him. The sun hadn't shown its face at all today, but now evening was settling in beyond the storm. Other than the displays for the radar and the radio he had on in the cockpit, the world would soon be pitch dark.

Was that a good thing? It would hide the waves that seemed to tower in every direction when he was in a trough, or go on forever as he crested the next. It was all beyond his control now. His life was in the hands of *Brise* and her sea anchor.

And if that wasn't enough? Lost at sea—who would know? At least that would be a familiar feeling.

Never good enough to make any impression on his narcissistic father.

The career that had blown up in his face...

He shut his eyes as he crested one last wave to shut out the vision. Even knowing that it might be too dark to see at all by the time he crested the next wave thirty seconds from now, he couldn't make himself look at his last glimpse of daylight.

He'd killed himself for John in his last job.

For twelve months, since the day after that trip with Teresa down the coast, he'd given John's firm his all. Each aspect of his job was a full-time proposition, yet together they were far more than that. John should have hired three people, maybe four, not counting the rest of the staff. But that hadn't stopped Ron from throwing himself body and soul to try and do it all.

Hero of the corporate save! Yeah, sure. How many times did you sell yourself that one, Ron?

The department he'd inherited with only a single remaining, benighted staffer had been a mission-critical step of the overall operation. It had taken four new staff and twenty-hour days not to miss their delivery deadlines. On top of that, their original operational flow would have pleased a Rube Goldberg fan. If there was a more awkward way to do each step of the necessary operations, Ron had no idea what they might be. Like they'd painted over the barnacles on a hull year after year rather than scraping it clean first. It had dragged like an old scow.

But before he could straighten *that* out, he had to fix the main problem. The core, hundred-thousand-dollar software package that made their department run, hadn't been upgraded in so long that the manufacturer neither supported nor offered training in it anymore.

Twelve months.

Ron rode the darkness down another wave face with only the dim glow of the boat's instruments casting any light. As planned he was barely making any way, held in place by his parachute anchor beneath the waves. The little half-knot of speed that he was making was going backwards, which didn't show on the meter. The compass said he was pointed east, into the waves and wind. But the storm was dragging him west, slowly, but at least toward his destination.

Unlike that damn job, though you were so sure it was, weren't you, you naive idiot?

Twelve months he'd given everything to that job, except for the rare occasions when he'd emerged to sail or outfit *Brise* right near the end he hadn't known was imminent.

And Teresa. Though nowhere near enough time spent with her.

He'd taken her on a few shakedown sails, mostly short

afternoon trips. But one time he'd taken two whole days off and run from Seattle up to Orcas Island. They'd eaten at the luxurious Rosario Resort, dining on Alaskan Snow Crab Pasta and Pan-Roasted Salmon with mushroom risotto—along with an eye-searing bill. But it had been a great date... before he'd had to spend half of the return sail burning up cell time to dig out a rush project, leaving the sailing to Teresa.

He'd barely seen her since except for stolen minutes.

Then the hammer had fallen.

John had strolled up to Ron's desk on a Tuesday afternoon, an hour before Ron's presentation to a major client that he'd had little to do with previously. They were unhappy and it had been decided that Ron was the one to talk them down.

John had veered him into HR and told him to sit down.

The HR person had been halfway through her spiel before Ron had figured out what was going on.

I'm being fired? Why?

Failure to achieve defined goals. She didn't know the details but it became clear that it was the failure to upgrade that core piece of software. Sure, all he'd needed was two weeks' help from the IT guys that John would never free up—followed by a week of quiet for dedicated training of the staff on the new product that was never going to happen.

That, of course, would be stated to any possible future employer calling for a reference. And the Seattle IT project management world wasn't a big community. Once word was out, he'd be a pariah. He hadn't been fired; he'd been blacklisted.

Such complete and total bullshit! Which didn't make it any less real.

Out of other ideas, he'd sold his car, canceled his slip rental at the marina—and set sail.

Real fucking brilliant, Ron!

Now thousands of kilometers away in the middle of the storm, the anger boiled so hot that he finally couldn't keep it down. He managed to lean over the cockpit coaming and heave up the burning bile onto the outer deck. The spray would wash it out the scuppers, if he could ever stop heaving it up.

And his big dream. He was out here in the middle of the fucking ocean, in the middle of his big dream, and it was that utter bastard John who'd set him on it. Not coherent thoughts or plans. Not hope or joy.

Ron went from wet heaves, to searing bile, and finally to dry heaves.

Christ! How far past all reason had he pushed himself? He sprawled with his elbows hooked over the coaming rail. That was all that kept him from sliding into the cockpit's footwell amid the sloshing seawater.

I get it! Alright already! I get it.

Why had it taken him so long? In retrospect, he could see that the betrayal had been a long time coming. He'd never asked why the department lead and the three others had all decided to find new jobs at roughly the same time. Probably wouldn't have been told the truth if he had.

He could even see that John had decided that rather than giving the upset client a presentation—that had caused Ron three sleepless nights to build because there simply wasn't any other time to do it—why not simply fire a department head for them?

John had found an excuse, put Ron's head on a platter, and then had probably served up Ron's presentation as his own.

"Bastard!" His throat tore as he laughed and quickly fell to crying.

Tomorrow, if the storm didn't find some way to kill him first, he'd start over. He'd begin his journey at some random point a thousand kilometers from anywhere.

For now? Rubbing at his eyes simply made them sting with excess salt water.

He was such a fucking mess. No wonder Teresa hadn't come to see him off when he said he was leaving.

5

———————

Crossing out of the storm toward Hawaii

For the three days of the storm Ron hadn't been able to keep down anything more solid than a fruit drink. It wasn't seasickness. His gut was simply wound in such a hard knot that it couldn't take in anything new.

The sea anchor, resisting the storm, had kept his drift in check. In those three days *Brise* had covered the same distance she would normally sail in eight hours.

Made it through. Safe past the storm.

After an hour spent fighting the sea anchor back aboard, he'd collapsed in simple exhaustion. For six hours straight the boat bobbed and weaved on the confused seas left behind by the storm, while he slept as if he *had* died in the storm.

This time he *did* wake up on the floor of cockpit where the motion of an unruly wave had tossed him.

Getting underway again, he began the four-thousand-kilometer haul on to Hawaii as the sky cleared and the seas settled. His course now lay well south of most shipping lanes. All the big boats had the power and urgency to ignore the best currents and winds as they simply powered along the shortest-distance great circle routes from Asia to America and back. Out here between Mexico and Hawaii, there were few intruders besides the recreational sailors.

He'd slept twenty of the next twenty-four hours and came out of it feeling half human and utterly famished.

He'd weathered his first major storm at sea, a big one. On his own. It had been utterly terrifying at times, but also good. Well...survivable.

Sure, I can solo around the world. I'm good enough. No prob! Talk about a fall from smugness. Brutal fucking storm.

He'd survived it as he would survive the collapse of his career. This was good. Maybe a fresh start was what he needed. Time away to...do...something.

For the next ten days he had plenty to keep him busy. Drying out and repacking the sea anchor. Two of the rigging lines had taken bad chafing during the storm. As he replaced them, he was able to figure out why. One he was able to fix himself, the other one he'd need to hit a marine supply store in Hawaii so that it wouldn't happen again.

He'd thought his life's possessions had been well stowed below. Half had been. Half had ended up flung about the cabin. As he'd waded through the mess to sort it out, he wondered why he'd thought most of it was so important.

Embrace the new life! Alice fell down the rabbit hole into Wonderland. Well, he'd climb back out before he got lost again.

He began a give-away pile on the settee.

The table stood in the middle of the cabin, less than a foot wide with both leaves folded down. Raised, it reached the curved settee for four to sit at one side and the straight bench for three to sit on the other. He'd spent most nights on the latter, a single-wide berth he could pitch into still fully clothed not three steps from the base of the ladder to the cockpit.

He still had yet to sleep in the double-wide v-berth up in the very bow of the boat. Those extra steps had seemed too far away from the pilot's station of instruments or the cockpit ladder. And that big forward bed had been the last place he and Teresa had made love before the final apocalypse at work that had cast him so adrift.

Soon the settee was covered with junk to give away. Like more saucepans than his three-burner stove had burners, and old science fiction books that he had on his e-reader anyway.

For the throw-away pile, he expanded onto the bench seat. Patch cables and adapters for computers he no longer even owned—a few so old that *no one* still owned them. A PS/2 cable had been ridiculous twenty years ago, and he couldn't even remember the last time he'd seen a DB25 serial cable. But what a DB37 was for he couldn't remember at all. Yet he had them aboard.

Stupid talismans of a past he'd clung onto for far to long. Done with that!

He unearthed a number of things, good, expensive things, that he'd bought a second time, forgetting he'd already bought them once. Maybe he could sell those. Not for much probably.

Then the boat took a wave hard and dumped everything onto the cabin floor and mixed it all up again. After going on deck to make sure everything was okay, he sorted the... *let's be honest*...jetsam into bags that he left on the cabin floor this time.

Finally, after sorting through everything in the various deck lockers, and the galley, master bedroom, and main cabin below, there was only one area left.

The Cheoy Lee 48's center-cockpit design had one more advantage beyond its place at the center of the boat. Having the cockpit shifted a third of the way forward had a significant impact on the interior layout. The galley and main cabin were less luxurious. The navigator's station, typically a comfortable sitting area to work radios, keep a log, and even an additional pilot's berth, was now a cramped seat.

The trade-off was the addition of a rear cabin.

He knew he should go back and sort through what was in there, but he kept finding other chores to avoid that. When he caught himself trying to understand a book on marlinspike rope work so that he could make a swim ladder from scratch, he knew he was being foolish.

For the first time since he'd left port, Ron made himself follow the narrow passage that ran aft from the galley along the port side. Once past the structure of the cockpit up above, it opened into a suite far more private than the forward v-berth off the main cabin. A big bed filled part of the space. It had numerous skylights and its own hatch to flood it with sunlight. Tucked neatly around the edges of the cockpit's shape above was a second bath, complete with head, sink, and shower. There was also a small desk.

Prior to his departure, it had been crammed with gear: spare sails, tools, anything he'd simply needed to get out of the way. But his first night out, anchored off the Port Townsend beach rather than going ashore, he'd properly stowed everything that had been jammed in here.

Now, other than a few pillows having been knocked about by the storm, the cabin was pristine. The drawers were empty except for a few odds and ends: pens, paper, a clip-on light for reading a book at night—the light was still bright when he checked the battery. The bookshelf held a dictionary and thesaurus, new copies of the same ones he'd seen over Teresa's desk in Seattle. The narrow closet held…

He dropped onto the bed and instantly knew why he'd avoided this cabin. And why he'd left it empty even though space was at such a premium.

A brand-new set of deep-sea foul weather gear hung in the closet. He'd bought them when he'd purchased his own —the same day he'd bought the sailboat. He didn't need to check the label to remember that it was a women's medium. Teresa's size.

He'd made a space for her on his boat.

And she'd love it. He knew her well enough to be sure of that.

He'd been able to see her here. Sitting in a tropical port, a light breeze drifting through the open portholes, working on her next book.

Ron had made a space for her on his boat.

But he hadn't made space for her in his life.

6

---

70 kilometers SSE of Honolulu

It was ringing.

Ron's radio could have been patched into a phone system to place this call at any time. But he'd delayed it until he could link to a Hawaiian cell tower. He didn't want to spread his shame all over the open airways, at least that's what he told himself.

Instead he'd stewed through five more days of sailing, sleeping almost as little as he had during the storm. The last eight hours, from when the towering summit of Mauna Kea had broken the horizon—his first sight of anything other than ocean in twenty-three days—until his phone had declared a single bar of signal, had been pure torture.

Then he'd delayed for another hour and five kilometers trying to figure out what to say. As if he hadn't done exactly that for the last five nights.

Second ring.

Third.

Oh crap! She wasn't going to pick up. She'd know it was him and—

"Hi, this is Teresa."

"Hey, it's me." Ron winced; she'd already know that.

Her voice continued. "I'm probably deep in solving a murder and I can't tear myself away. Or I'm in editing hell and can't face anyone. Leave your name and the title of your favorite book." Her voicemail beeped.

Hell! And damnation! And the curse of the sunken continent of Mu besides!

"I...uh... I didn't want to do this on voicemail. I'm...crap!" But maybe he was going to anyway. "I never asked. I should have asked. You know. If you wanted to come with me. Honestly I don't know what's wrong with me, so I'm hoping that you do. I'm coming up on Maui. Um, I'm fine. I hit a terrible storm, but *Brise* was a total champ. Exactly like you said, she made it a breeze. Okay, that was a white lie but none of it was her fault. And uh..." What? *Think, Ron. Think.* "My favorite book is you. Okay. Stupid and corny. Too corny for one of your books. But it's true. I miss you so much. No. That's not right. I mean yes I do. I really do. But it's more than that. What I mean to say—"

The beep cut him off.

"Shit!"

7

———————

Lahaina Harbor
Maui, Hawaii

He kept his phone close and he kept it charged—it didn't ring.

Twenty-four hours. That's how long it took him from deciding that he couldn't call her back without getting all stalkery, to reaching the back side of Maui.

There'd been no sleep—again.

Sailing solo ain't so attractive now, is it, buddy boy?

Close around the Hawaiian Islands there were far too many boats to trust the autopilot. There also wasn't a lot of sea room here—it would be far too easy to run into an island while he slept. Instead of standing out to sea and turning about, he brewed coffee and kept watch.

The Vic-Maui International Yacht Race always landed in Lahaina Harbor. Twenty-five days ago he'd passed Victoria Harbor as he headed out the Strait of Juan de Fuca. The race winners would cover the same ground in half that time. Of course many of them would be in lean racing boats with full crews pushing the boat ahead every hour of the day and night.

He'd had offers to crew the Vic-Maui or the much longer return trip. What was two weeks downwind was a five- to six-week return, usually done by a pick-up crew. The skipper/owner would fly back to the Northwest, returning to their cushy day job, while the crew beat north until they could pick up the high Japanese Current and sweep down the Canadian coast.

But he'd never been able to justify the time off. All the years he'd lived on the West Coast and he'd never made it to Hawaiian Islands at all. Well now he had.

Welcome to Maui.

The water was the color he'd seen in a thousand photos but it was also something else entirely. The interplay of blues and turquoise was vibrantly alive in a way no photo could capture.

The birds. After weeks at sea without a single sighting, the birds were a shock, he hadn't missed that they were gone until they were back. A shearwater dove for fish. A white egret lofted by as casually as someone's grandparent. Ducks with brilliant red sides that he didn't recognize were busy along the shore. Small fish left circular rings on the smooth waters as they nipped bugs from the surface. The air and the water were vibrant with life.

It was evening as he sailed in close to Lahaina, lowered sails, and started the motor for the first time in three weeks.

As he nosed toward the small harbor behind the big rock breakwater, the sun was sliding behind Lanai, the next island to the west. Already the turquoise was shifting to pick up the golds in the sky.

A coffee-klatch of pintail ducks scowled at him as they paddled aside when he passed too close.

He'd already prepped this lines and hung the fenders off the side, but there was still a lot to do all at once as he nosed carefully between the channel markers. According to the chart it had been dredged to two fathoms, twelve feet. But the harbor itself was only eight and he drew six-and-a-half. He should be safe at any tide, but he had no idea if he had inches or feet of leeway.

Check the tides first. Lesson for next time.

Past the channel markers, it quickly shoaled to three feet. *Brise* would not be happy if he drifted there.

Small sailboats flocked by, unconcerned by the shallows. A parasailing boat came off the beach, and raced off for a final evening run.

Made it! But he didn't like the question that followed immediately after, *Why?*

Lahaina Harbor, Lahaina, Maui, Hawaii.

It was the sort of place couples came for romantic getaways. Not the touristy types who massed at the big hotels and the thousand tacky boutiques designed to gather as much mainland money as possible and keep it in the islands. No, here the pace would be slower.

He and Teresa had talked about coming here. Okay, *he* had talked about it. He'd ride down the Vic-Maui, or come here to pick up a boat for the return. He hadn't considered stopping anywhere else in Hawaii as he'd now circled clear of the Big Island and bypassed the rest of Maui to land at its westernmost point. This had simply been where he would come.

It did have the advantage of placing the mainland on the far side of the islands. He'd have to backtrack, pass the islands once more to head east toward home. So, from here he could launch *west* with that extra little barrier pushing him ahead toward the rest of the world.

Where?

Japan? Fiji? Guam? The Solomons?

It didn't matter. He'd stop here, top off his water tanks, and get fresh produce. He hadn't used any fuel, except to motor into the harbor here. Past that?

He wouldn't think about it.

The inner harbor was crazy. He was used to long sets of finger piers reaching out to either side of a primary dock.

Not here.

Lahaina Harbor was too small for that. It was a boulder-walled rectangle with mooring down both sides. Boats were rafted up side-to-side. Power boats were all parked stern in. The sailboats were all bow in. It would be dicey to pull it off single-handed. Not only did he have to come to a perfect stop with the bow at the edge of the perimeter walkway, but he'd also have to pick up one of the buoys floating out in the middle of the harbor to tie off his stern. All while manipulating the controls from the central cockpit.

Maybe he'd leave and anchor off the beach. Later he could come ashore in his dinghy if he had the energy. Or maybe tomorrow. It didn't matter.

He managed to make a three-point turn between the two lines of boats without snagging any of the mid-channel buoys. His was definitely on the large side for this harbor. There were a couple of sixty-foot power yachts and several tourist boats with massive "Whale Watch" signs painted down the sides. But the common class here, in both sail and power, was down in the thirty-foot range.

Give it up! Anchor off the beach. Deal with life tomorrow.

Ron was easing back out of the harbor. Full dark was settling and he was cursing himself for not having anchored out in the *roads,* as the offshore stretches were called, to begin with.

A shout. He eased off the throttle and looked around.

"Aloha the sailboat!" He finally spotted the man standing at the end of the service pier and waved to show that he heard.

The man began gesturing him over.

He didn't need to fuel up now, but the gestures were insistent.

Ron had drifted past the dock, but easing into reverse, he crossed the rudder and slowly backed until he was turned and alongside the slip.

"No one else coming in here tonight," the man said as he leaned out to grab the line that Ron had preset along the gunwale. "Probably not tomorrow either. They can always use the other side of the pier."

With relief, Ron eased to a stop and hopped down to help tie off the boat.

He almost pitched off the other side of the pier because it didn't rock, unlike the boat.

The man laughed. "How long at sea?"

"Seattle." Ron braced his feet apart, but the pier didn't stop swaying though it was anchored to the sea bed. It was making him dizzy.

"Give it a day. Go for a swim. That'll set you up good."

Ron had heard about sea legs, but never been aboard a boat long enough to develop them before. He staggered up and down the dock securing *Brise* like a drunk in a hurricane. On land was the first time he'd felt queasy with seasickness in the whole trip.

Crawling back aboard, he made it as far as the cockpit. Stretching out on one of the benches, he stared up at the stars that had come out without his noticing. They'd all shifted strangely. Cygnus and Lyra, instead of being directly overhead were far to the north. As the sky continued to darken, the Milky Way put in an appearance far higher in the sky than he was used to.

His body begged for sleep.

But all his brain could do was think about Teresa not returning his call.

8

Lahaina Harbor
Maui, Hawaii

Ron bolted upright in the cockpit.

"I need a crew!"

He hadn't slept, but the moment of the dawn had brought absolute clarity.

He staggered down the dock, his balance about halfway back to normal for being off the sea, yet much worse for massive sleep derivation. That's why he needed a crew. The lack of sleep on the solo passage hadn't been safe. During that storm, he'd been lucky to not hallucinate a Seattle sidewalk and step of his boat into the ocean. He'd need a crew so that he could make the return run to Seattle fast.

By the time the service dock attendant who'd helped him last night showed up, he'd already filled half of the harbor's small Dumpster. He'd also found the *Free Stuff* shelf in the harbor office, which was unlocked, and buried it in his castoffs. There was always somewhere for boaters to exchange books or pass on old gear when new gear was acquired. He'd wager the bulk of his would be cleared out before the end of the day.

The few others who came off the boats to get breakfast in town offered him an *Aloha* and a wide berth.

Okay. Rationality running low. Definitely needed to refill that...somehow.

"I need a crew," he croaked out as soon as the attendant strolled up. He was a big guy with an easy smile, a brown-and-white Hawaiian shirt, and a trim beard gone half gray.

"Ease down, *brah.* Ease down. You've only just arrived." The man settled into a plastic chair in front of the office, a massive to-go coffee cup in his hand with the drawing of a mule on it. Below the drawing it said, *Bad Ass Coffee.* So, he held a massive to-go cup with the drawing of an *ass* on it.

Ron blinked to refocus. It didn't work until he'd done it a few times. He couldn't remember the man's name. He took a deep breath, but didn't feel any calmer.

"I need a crew, Akamu." Apparently a part of him had caught the guy's name last night.

"But—"

"A racing crew. Need the speed. Three at least." Ron sounded a little hysterical, even to himself. "Today would be really good."

"Where are you headed in such a hurry?"

"Seattle."

Akamu looked at him strangely. Then he glanced over at the stern of *Brise* as if checking his memory. Below the boat's name was the port of registry, Seattle, Washington, USA.

"You gone *lolo, brah?*"

Ron didn't need Akamu's expression to know he sounded like a crazy man.

"I—" It was stupid but, hey, since when was that news. "There's a girl. A woman. I left her behind. In Seattle." He held up his phone as if it meant something. Oh, it did. "She won't answer."

"*Shoots!*" Akamu acknowledged with a nod. He drank from his coffee cup as if there wasn't a reason in the world to hurry.

"I need—"

Akamu held up a hand to stop him.

Ron bit his tongue.

"Vic-Maui is next month, *brah*. The boat-bum return crews are starting to filter in, but they have come early to enjoy Hawaii."

In the sailing community, boat bum wasn't the insult it sounded. There were plenty of people who *bummed* a ride on various boats as a way of life for a summer or a year. They traded their crew skills for food and a free, if not fast, lift. If they were lucky, maybe enough spending money when they were done to hold them over until they found the next boat.

The Vic-Maui race was one of the hot rides because the owners desperately needed crew for the long haul of sailing their boats back to the Pacific Northwest. It was one of the longest races in the world that wasn't simply traveling a circle so that the boat and crew ended up where they'd started. It was over twice the length of the Newport Bermuda Race, the other big ride for a boat bum.

Meaning he'd never find a crew unless he paid. Money he didn't really have. He'd sold his house for a lot more money than his boat, but that was supposed to support him for the long ride around the world. Which was years.

He dropped into a chair beside Akamu and stared at *Brise*. A typical circumnavigation by sail, without pushing, taking time to see places he was passing through, took three or four years.

That number hadn't really sunk in.

Had Teresa understood the scale of what he was doing? Probably. She was much better at that sort of thing than he was. She saw the consequences before he even understood the action.

Like a grown up. Silently telling himself to shut up? *Nope, didn't help.*

Maybe he should go home to Seattle. Give up the trip. Try to patch things up, if she'd let him.

"You could fly."

But if he did, would he ever come back? His dream floated fifty feet away. If he returned to Seattle? He could feel himself calling a boat broker in a few months to ship home his belongings and get what he could for the boat.

He now knew that the stories were true. Supposedly the cheapest places to buy a cruising boat were in the tropical paradises: Hawaii, Fiji, and Tahiti. Sailors set out and, unable to sustain their dreams, ultimately abandoned their boats.

Even after a few weeks' break, if he crawled back into the corporate grinder, some part of him would die.

Nope! Not the right answer.

"Where do I post signs?" he asked Akamu. Because the dream of sailing solo around the world was a naive one. He *could* do it, but what would be the point? He'd have stories that no one other than another deep-sea sailor would want to hear. And then what?

"Well," Akamu offered reluctantly, "there's a notice board at the head of the dock here. You might try down at the yacht club. You a member of another club, Seattle or something? They have these reciprocity agreements with a lot of places, if you're a member of one club, the other will let you in. Maybe use their e-mail list."

Ron laughed in Akamu's face and then had to explain. "The Seattle Yacht Club has a twenty-grand initiation fee, plus annual dues. You need multiple references from other members and it can take a year to be approved. I belong to the Sloop Tavern Yacht Club."

"Maybe they—"

"Their total annual fee is ninety dollars a year, fifty-five if you don't have a boat. It's traditional to buy a round for the bar when you pay your fee, which costs far more."

"Now *that* sounds like a proper yacht club!" Akamu joined in his laugh.

It felt good. Even with the lack of sleep and his flurry of activity this morning cleaning out the boat, that brief shared laugh felt good. What would it be like to sit here for a day? Or a week? Lay on a beach with a book for a day. There must be amazing wildlife and nature to see here. Hell, there's volcanos.

Maybe the dream wasn't dead. But alone? That wasn't right either.

He slouched in the chair and closed his eyes as Akamu chatted with some other boater in no hurry at all. Ron felt the warm sun at his back as it climbed over the shoulder of those big volcanos that had built the island. He'd never seen an active volcano before. Mt. St. Helens had exploded before he was born though the locals still talked about it like it was yesterday. It would be nice to see that. Maybe even tour the observatory atop one of the peaks. Sail around the other islands and see what else there was to see.

The other boater wandered away.

"Yes, *braddah,* sometimes you must simply sit and wait," Akamu said thoughtfully.

Ron didn't bother looking at him, or even opening his eyes. He could hear people returning from breakfast. There was slow-building flutter of noise. He half-blinked his eyes and saw them gathering under an *Atlantis Submarine Tour* sign.

The dock was alive, but it was all background. Muted. The long nights had caught up and he was almost asleep in his chair before Akamu spoke again.

"Maybe the goddess Laka is watching over you and *this* pretty lady wants to sail on your boat."

"Maybe," a voice from a dream.

He knew that voice. "Teresa," maybe he'd stay in this happy dream for awhile.

"Yes?"

He jolted upright and looked at her. He tried to shout, but was afraid that she was an apparition of Akamu's goddess. He began to reach out but feared she might be no more than a sleep-deprivation induced hallucination.

Teresa stood slightly hipshot, propping up a large backpack that rested beside her. Electric red sneakers with no socks and long legs to black denim shorts. She wore a red t-shirt he'd bought for her, showing an old typewriter and a scrolled out piece of paper stating, *I'm plotting a murder.* Her mop of unruly hair a dark blonde cap of curls. Honey-colored eyes and her smile...

"You're here." It was little more than a gasp.

Her smile grew.

"You're *really* here. You came."

Akamu chuckled but didn't interrupt.

"To sail?"

She shrugged and he didn't know what to say to that.

He looked at Akamu who rolled his eyes at him. Ron still didn't get it.

Finally Teresa took pity on him, as he recalled she often had to do.

She took a step closer, letting her pack flop down onto the dock and set her computer bag on top of it—both were stuffed to the gills.

"You have to remember to *ask*."

He'd never actually asked if she would sail with him.

Too afraid that the answer would be no? Or because he was a complete idiot?

Didn't matter.

She was here.

Here with that big pack and her laptop bag. She'd always said she could write anywhere as long as she had her computer and a supply of caffeine-free diet Coke. He had plenty of the latter on board though he rarely drank it himself.

Ron struggled to his feet. When he brushed at her cheek, she leaned into it. When he kissed her, she kissed him back so gently that it was far more promise than anything physical.

"I need to ask. Right. I'll," he had to clear his throat again to speak. "I'll keep that in mind for the future."

This time the kiss was a promise for a long future ahead.

RETURN PASSAGE

ABOUT THIS STORY

*A musician seeks inspiration on the open sea
and finds it in the most unexpected way.*

Myles and Rose are twins. Despite the success of their musical duet, they can't manage to break out. Myles knows they're missing something if only he could pin it down.

Vonda's attempts to restart her life keep sinking beneath the waves. She needs to chart a new course.

A chance meeting on Maui and a leisurely five-week sailboat ride to Victoria, Canada changes the future for all three of them.

1

The hull creaked as the submarine *Atlantis* slipped beneath the waves. They sat in sideways-facing seats made of plastic darker blue than the ocean depths. In front of each seat were big round portholes to observe the Hawaiian reefs in all of their glorious color. Sunbeams struck down through crystal blue waters as if they'd entered a particularly soothing space warp.

Forty tourists sat in two out-facing rows down the length of the single cabin. The two pilots and the guide were perched up at the bow.

"Wild!" Rose whispered from behind him. They'd chosen back-to-back seats in the twenty-meter-long submarine so that, between them, they wouldn't miss anything.

But Myles Lauer was too busy listening to the music of it to notice much else. The sub made a hell of song descending to cruise the reefs off western Maui.

Ping. Ping, Creak. The hull set an atmosphere of tension as the water pressure compressed the hull. Not loud enough to be unnerving, but it let him know they were entering another world. How to translate that into a song?

Welcome to somewhere you've never been before.

He'd often couldn't pin down the answers, but he liked to keep feeding his subconscious ideas to play with.

The tour guide spoke with that lazy lilt of Hawaii that always made life sound so much fun. Little dabs of pidgin only added to the rhythm and the feeling.

"Check it out, you folks on the starboard. See dat eel under the blue coral fan giving us the stink eye? He be a real moke, you go divin', you don't want to screw with him. On the port, remember that's the left side, see the blacktip reef shark? He's brown with black tips on his fins. He's truly a sweetheart. Five feet, this is a big one. Lives on little fishes and maybe crabs. He no mess with you if you no mess with him."

The sunlight shifted, fading only a little as the forty-five-minute tour took them deeper. But that was Rose's thing. She saw colors in ways he couldn't imagine. She's the one who brought the harmonies to their music.

New melodies always surrounded Myles at every turn, like how the schools of fish swirled by the porthole glass. A small cluster of black-and-white-striped Moorish Idols with splashes of sunshine yellow that looked like someone had spilled the final color over parts their white by accident. A refrain so predictable that everyone's ready to sing along, hit with a splash of Rose's harmony? Maybe a twist in the final line of each repeat. *Yeah, like that.*

A school of purple triggerfish swirled by like a high riff, scattering from the plodding bass of a solo green sea turtle, lazing over the reef. The coral offered up accent notes in orange, white, blue, gold. Sprays of fantastical fans rose above the stable touchstone backbeat of the globular brain coral.

He barely noticed the supposed highlight of the dive. The sub company had sunk an aged steel replica of an even older wooden schooner that had been a whaling museum for years. The original had actually spent its working life as a trade ship until it was cast in the whaling role for Michener's *Hawaii.* Now its replica was an artificial reef with fifteen years of growth on it. Bottom line, it wasn't as old as it looked. Fish and coral grew on it. No rousing through-line of story or rollicking chorus, at least not one that he could find.

As the sub circled at its lazy walking pace to reveal the ship to the passengers on the other side, he stared out across the sandy plain. Maybe Rose would see something in the wreck that he didn't. In the midst of the busy emptiness there was a sudden disturbance. A ray flapped up out of the sand, creating a cloud of fine grit in the water, then breaking free of the cloud like a sailboat emerging from a squall line.

Revealed, it had three-meter-wide wings of black covered in white polka dots. The beat of its wings were as slow and lazy as the turtle's. Too slow. Myles wanted up-tempo. He wanted energy. Yet that rippling wingbeat rang clear as a pulse in his head.

Their duo made their money in playing bar gigs. Packing the dance floors all over Seattle from the Tractor Tavern to the J&M had made them popular, but they couldn't find the next level. They should be playing Q Nightclub or Supernova Seattle. At Bumbershoot they never got near the main stages unless they were down front with the other dancers. And national tours? They'd only done one of the Western Washington county fairs.

"That pod of pilot whales was so cool," Rose spoke as

they filed out of the sub, climbing to the deck, and crossing over to the waiting speedboat to return them to the harbor.

"What whales?" He actually didn't remember anything much since watching that ray rise up out of the sand. There must be something there, but the beat was odd.

"That pod that circled the sub three times wondering if the sub was a new kind of whale."

Myles looked down at the water off the side as Rose laughed at him. Nothing to see despite the clear water. He shrugged at her. His twin sister always knew that he got lost in his head.

2

———

The Dirty Monkey was prime dancing turf in Lahaina.

They'd pre-arranged to play a three-night series here before they'd flown from Seattle to Maui. This trip was a creative break, but playing a gig also gave them an excuse to write it off on their taxes. In truth, the two-month break was because Myles was going insane going nowhere—career limbo.

Time for something completely different.

Two weeks kicking around the Maui paradise and then ferry a sailboat back to Victoria, British Columbia. The annual Vic-Maui Yacht Race had left BC for the two-week hustle down the trade winds to Lahaina Harbor at about the same time he and Rose had stepped on a plane in Seattle. There'd be a hell of a party after the race, and then volunteer return crews would board the boats to sail them back, while the owners and race crews hopped their flights home.

For the return crews it was a long slow ride north to catch the Japanese Current and slide across then down to Victoria Harbor. A five-week luxury ride they'd done seven times over the years. The first time had been between junior and senior year of high school for their next-door neighbor. No need to own a boat, just deliver it home in one piece. Sweet!

They wrote a lot of music on those long rides, yet another argument for the tax man on why it should be a write-off.

The Dirty Monkey was anything but. It was in the heart of Lahaina and the bar filled the second floor of a Front Street building. Big windows opened onto a balcony overlooking the narrow two-lane with wide sidewalks. It was a walking kind of town, for both tourists and locals. Hopefully that meant it was a dancing kind of town.

It had none of the funk feel of most of the places they usually played. The fake white marble bar was surrounded by steel stools. The floor had high-top tables that could seat six, or a dozen crowded around if they were standing. Behind the bar was a wide selection of beer taps and bottled liquor. Especially whiskey—they had lots of that.

Their wood floor showed heavy wear, the kind that came from a serious amount of dancing. Tonight VMR's music would be pumping out the windows.

He and Rose had named their band for *Very Myles and Rose*. Or maybe *Very Much Reality!* Or... They kept thinking up new acronyms—they couldn't even settle on their name, never mind what brand would make their careers really take off.

Myles had loved the energy of performing since he was born, at least that's how Dad told it. Every time he said it, Mom would rub her belly as if it hurt, *Started way before birth, honey!* Myles had dragged his much shyer twin sister along for the ride.

It had all sorts of advantages beyond how their music fit together.

They received so many compliments from strangers on what a good-looking couple they were, that they'd stopped correcting people except when it mattered.

They couldn't have looked much more different and still had the same parents. But at their senior prom he'd won Handsomest Prince to stand beside Beautifulest Princess. Neither of their dates had been surprised or much begrudged them that. He'd taken after Dad's fair and blond. Big sister Rose, all of eleven minutes older, had Mom's darker coloring and long mahogany hair framing a narrow face. Both five-eleven, they looked like blond and brown bookends.

Another advantage was when he was about to do something stupid with a girl, Rose could snag his elbow with a, *Come along, dear.* If she had a guy she couldn't shed, Myles would walk off with her hand-in-hand.

They had a mutual support pact that had seen each through a lot of challenging times.

And the music. Myles knew they were good. The penny had dropped, dime, nickel, and quarter too. But the silver dollar wouldn't fall. They made a living, but it was a good thing they shared an apartment and preferred a pub meal to a steak house for the rare meal out.

He pulled out his travel guitar. Little more than the fretboard and bridge carved out of maple with the tuning machines tucked into the small body of the instrument, it weighed three pounds and fit in the overhead bin on an airplane. Hell, it was small enough, he could plug in headphones and *play* on an airplane without disturbing anyone.

Rose slung on her traveling bass, all of six inches longer. They plugged into the bar's sound system and began to play.

They'd had a lot of trial and error on what worked and what didn't. Originally they'd warm up the crowd with a few mellow songs, get the audience used to the shift to live music, then hit them with a dance beat.

Not anymore. It was early yet, but fifteen people in a bar that could hold a hundred was a thin crowd. Still...

Myles double-checked that the doors over the street were open, and nodded for Rose to punch into one of their hotter dance riffs. It was a long thing with no words. Rose had found an irresistible heavy beat and he'd built a playful melody onto it, like a cat chasing a windup mouse. Even in an audience of two, it set people dancing.

By the time they finished it, half the bar was dancing, which was now more like forty people. The owner was too busy with drink orders to even shoot them a smile, exactly the way he'd want to be.

It was deep in their second set when he noticed her—dramatic as hell.

It wasn't her height, a leggy five-eight. Or her crazy Hawaiian head scarf that covered her hair, including her eyebrows, like she was a woman of mystery. In the dim light of the evening, there was no way to tell anything about much about her build. Slender, maybe, and far enough to the back that she kept disappearing from view.

Still, she was incredible to watch.

Her dance moves weren't star-dancer amazing, but her timing was out of this world.

With her body, she wove a counterpoint around Myles' own melody as if he were the one playing the supporting bassline. He shifted the next verse and she wove back to his original melody as if teasing him for abandoning it. Rose looked at him, Myles could feel it, but he stayed focused on the dancer.

Not really watching the stage or her own place in the crowd, she and Myles played a game anyway. Her knee would find Rose's backbeat, picking out that F-sharp three-below-middle-C every time the bass ventured there. He'd written this number in G-major with a I-V-vi-IV—G, D, E-minor, C—chord progression as a tongue-in-cheek homage to the *most overused sensitive female progression* in pop music.

Then the woman's elbow would pick up the low E but on an off-rhythm accented by a head shaking G. When he moved to match, she slid into Rose's low C with a two-footed thump, and then started building again. Rose slid underneath their melody and harmony like she was laying down the world's oceans for their hull and sails to best ride on.

Between the three of them, they built the night layer upon layer. No more set breaks. The floor packed tighter than a mosh pit. At one point the bartenders were up and dancing on the bar top.

When the end came, it wasn't planned or orchestrated, it was simply the final note of how the night fit together. They returned to that first dance instrumental, but embellished and built in ways that reflected their three-way dance to the music.

By the last chord, the crowd was exhausted, ecstatic, and dancing each to their own beats of music as they stormed the bar.

That's when he made his mistake and glanced at Rose. They grinned at each other like two lost fools.

By the time he turned back, the scarfed dancer was gone.

3

———

"I swear to God she was real," Myles knew he was repeating himself pointlessly. His voice died flat against the cave's walls.

"God, Myles, drop it."

For a change of pace to their last day on Hawaii, they'd rented scooters and were circling Maui. Rose had turned at the sign for the Hana Lava Tube and now they were inside it and it was eating his sound. The entry fee included a flashlight and there were self-guided tour signs along the way.

He tended to breeze by those and then plague Rose to tell him the story as she read each one to the last comma and period. She was countering that by reading halfway, laughing at something, then finishing and walking away without a word. Which meant he'd have to read it himself— and it *was* interesting. By the third or fourth sign, he was skimming them for himself, then his sister would laugh and he'd have to backtrack to figure out why. She was right of course.

The lava that had formed this tube a thousand years ago had layered thickly over the top. Most of the ceiling was sixty feet or more thick and topped with soil and tropical growth madness outside.

After entering through a narrow opening and descending a flight of stairs, they were soon in the quarter-mile long tube. Big enough that even claustrophobes wouldn't have an issue and long enough that the other people there didn't make it feel crowded.

Part of that was because the wall ate up all of the sound. No long echoes in the Hana Lava Tube. Inside the vast tube, their voices were strangely dead. Whispers didn't carry five feet. He felt as if he had to shout a little to hear his own voice at all.

"It's the rock," Rose had always paid more attention in science class than he had. "It's so porous that the sound gets lost in it like commercial baffling."

"Fine. I'll use some to build our next sound booth." They had a small three-bedroom apartment and the third room had been lined with old quilts they'd picked up at garage sales. It made for a colorful recording studio. Too bad that neither of them were yet satisfied with the music they were producing so that they could release any of it.

"Do that!" Rose snapped, clearly sick of him. She had a point, he was fairly sick of himself. Starting tomorrow they'd be out on the sea. There he could just chill and fall into the routines of sailing, eating, and sleeping. If they caught a storm, they caught one, but there wasn't any heavy weather predicted. If they didn't he'd write music.

They'd sung two more nights at The Dirty Monkey, packed 'em in tight. But they'd never hit the deep groove again. It was like he'd been offered a peek of that next-level sound, his nose pressed to the proverbial window as he hung onto the ledge by his very fingernails.

But he couldn't sustain it and was once again mortal. And the fall hurt as assuredly as if it had been physical.

A good crowd but not all dancing. A happy owner, the first night's success had spread by word of mouth, but the next night there were almost as many drinking as there were dancing. No bartenders dancing on the marble bar top.

Not without...*her*.

"She wasn't a phantom or a phantasm or a poltergeist or imaginary or any of that."

Rose's look said he'd crossed over that edge where his sister always shifted into neutral mode. She wasn't going to react to or offer anything until he chilled. They both agreed that she'd laid down the hottest bass lines of her life, but she insisted that she'd only been taking her cues from him—if that didn't beat all.

"Maybe you were seeing her subconsciously..." Because if she had been, then the mystery dancer had indeed been real.

Rose's look told him that she'd been following his lead and he was badly overreaching. But if he had been imagining the dancer, then why hadn't he been able to find the music again on subsequent nights.

"Fine. I'll just focus on the lava tube."

"Finally," Rose's tone was rich with disbelief that it might last longer than any other subject had from the last three days.

Not another word. He wouldn't bring up the mystery dancer—now MD in his thoughts—ever again.

Besides, it was their last day on Maui. The Vic-Maui sailboats were in, the big finisher's party was tonight. Tomorrow, they'd meet the skipper for the handoff to the return crews and they'd be out on the high seas. Giving up on Lahaina, they were cruising the hundred-mile loop around the island. His chances of meeting MD the mystery dancer ever again were diminishing by the minute.

And the lava tube *was* interesting. The surfaces kept changing. One area was all sharp 'a'ā. It prickled his palm when he touched it, and it gulped up the sound of a tongue-click or finger-snap like a dog eating steak. Pāhoehoe layered over other surfaces in smooth twisty ropes. One chamber was thick with the stuff, like someone had poured milk chocolate on all the walls and ceiling. Sound didn't disappear on this texture. In fact, he kept catching licks and hints of the music they'd played that first night.

Not in his voice. Not in Rose's smooth alto. But—

And it was gone before he could ask if Rose heard it. Just a cluster of notes, flitting through his messed-up brain probably created because he wanted that next whatever-it-was so badly.

It was agony to have created, but to no longer quite able to hear what he'd done.

Because he hadn't done it alone.

Not even with Rose.

It was—right back where he started—MD.

He was blinking hard at the daylight as they emerged from the cool depths back into the heat of the day. Again, he'd missed whole portions of the adventure as he'd tried to grab onto those lost melodies that haunted him.

The heat and humidity were a hard slap after an hour underground. Mid-July was actually a crap time to be hanging out on Maui, but it wasn't his call when the Vic-Maui ran. It wasn't like Florida hideous, but it was more than his Seattle blood was used to.

"Let's head back."

Rose didn't point out that they were already doing that, having gone two-thirds around the island. She also was kind enough to not point out that he wasn't going to find MD.

4

Vonda Decosta emerged from the Red Ti Botanical Garden Maze, slightly dizzy from the constant direction changes, not that it was that hard a maze. Her metabolism was *so* screwed up.

The lava tube had been cool, but she'd been all goosebumps and wishing for a parka by the end of the underground walk. Humming to distract herself had helped...a little. A leisurely walk in the sun-saturated hedge maze had been what the doctor ordered—with a few less turns. She cleared her head with a final shake.

Doctor ordered! There was a phrase she could finally purge from her soul—fingers and toes crossed.

At the southern edge of the park that included the Hana Lava Tube, they'd built a maze out of red ti trees. They had big, lush-red leaves as long as her forearm that grew as thickly as a hedge. Shaped into a solid wall from knee-high to several feet over her head, they defined the passages but let the sun pour down.

As she'd wandered the paths, ignoring the little map, not

caring if she dead-ended here or retraced her steps there, she played with the music.

She'd forgotten how much she'd missed the music of her college *a cappella* days until it had reached out through the open windows of The Dirty Monkey and dragged her off the street. For the first time in a year, she'd stopped thinking, stopped worrying. For the first time in the years since college, she'd simply given herself up to the music.

And way the hell overdone it.

Jesus, Vonda! You gotta be more careful.

She was supposed to be over all this. Three months of chemo. Two-to-one recovery time meant six more months of climbing out of the hole that the chemicals and radiation had driven her into. She'd done all that and yet felt completely strung out from a single night of dancing.

How long are you gonna wallow?

A week ago, she'd have answered, *forever.*

The disease.

Then quitting her job to focus on her wellness.

Next her fiancé hadn't been able to deal with the future of a woman in her twenties who'd already had stage-two cancer. He'd kept emphasizing the *two* until she'd have probably thrown him out if he hadn't already left.

Now, as clean as they could test six months after end of treatment.

None of that had mattered. He'd been gone while she'd been still shaking from the second dose of chemo.

To hell with him and to hell with her past.

If the disease hadn't been what exhausted her, perhaps it was that she hadn't rebuilt her stamina at all.

Yet exhausting herself past reason wasn't the only thing that had happened that night.

Sure, she'd slept hard most of the day after that dance,

but it hadn't been mere exhaustion or the muscles so unused to the workout. She'd been caught in the trap for a year: diagnosis, second opinions, treatment, and recovery. Somehow, in that one blissful, passed-out sleep, she'd walked out the other side of the trap and left it behind.

Vonda knew about the *now,* right down deep in a way no always-healthy person could know. The time to make choices and changes was right now. It was *always* right now. Learn and grow. The dance had heaved overboard all that crap past; poor-ass choice of fiancé included.

Head scarves? Done!

She tugged it off her head and ran her fingers through the three inches of dark-blonde that had finally grown out. The warm breeze washing over the botanic garden with all of its foreign tropical sweetness caressed her scalp anew. Maybe she'd get some mousse and spike it. Dye it purple? Wouldn't *that* put her parents in a twist? Actually, Mom would probably go to the salon with her and get a color to match.

Christ but she'd be dead without them. Last thing they needed was their grown daughter re-intruding on their lives, but they'd been there for her every step of the way. Mom sympathized and coddled her. Dad didn't say much, but had become her go-to for wheels when she had the hundred-thousandth doctor's appointment. He was also the one who'd suggested she go to Hawaii for a break to celebrate the *supposed* end of recovery. Did it in his normally voluble way of slipping a plane ticket across the dinner table. Without a word, of course, but he did it.

Kicking me out? Vonda had asked.

Mom had made consoling sounds, as surprised as she was. Dad had shrugged a maybe. Not that he wanted her gone, but maybe that it was time.

And he'd been right. It was time to do things new and different.

She'd been here long enough to find her favorite beach. And yesterday, after sleeping away the day before, she'd spent bodysurfing on Slaughterhouse Beach up the coast. Backed by a steep cliff, and fronted by a snorkeling reef where she'd teased clown fish and carefully avoided a giant green sea turtle, she'd soaked up sun on the sand and cooled off under the trees. Such a blessing to be outdoors.

Today she was touring the sections of the island she hadn't seen in her three weeks here. Time to stretch herself.

Tomorrow? Who knew.

As she crossed from the maze back to the parking lot, she saw the two musicians from The Dirty Monkey heading there from the lava tube. She'd slept through their second show and been too enamored of the sunset on Slaughterhouse Beach to go to the third.

They were already on their scooters and tugging on helmets. She wanted to thank them, but it would sound stupid. Too...she didn't know what.

But as her feet remained rooted to the spot and they started their engines with a quick little splutter, she knew that was the old her. The one who had become so fragile that all action was terrifying.

"Hey! Wait!" The man pulled away without hearing, but the woman turned to look in her direction. She couldn't remember their names. She hadn't even looked at the poster by the door. Vonda had been walking the street looking for somewhere to have dinner and ended up on the dance floor with no conscious transition.

"Hey, yourself." The woman looked so amazing, all tall and elegant. Her shining hair far longer than Vonda had ever grown her own. All of the things that Vonda wasn't.

"You two were amazing the other night!" She blurted it out like a total fan girl.

"Thanks," the woman smiled. It wasn't something she'd done very often that night. At the bar she'd been the consummate chill bass player, cool and sexy beyond words or music.

"I missed the last two nights. When are you playing again?" Because she was so ready to shed more of her past.

The smile faded. "Six weeks until our next gig, sorry."

"Oh," she could feel her own smile die. Six weeks? Would she still be here then? Probably not. She'd been in day-to-day mode, but there was an energy now. A desire to move ahead. Except she wasn't sure what that meant anymore. Back to her old job? Legal secretary had paid the bills, but she didn't exactly miss it—like at all!

"If you're in Seattle, we'll be at a place called the High Dive."

"Oh! I live in Seattle."

The woman looked down the road after her lover, husband, whatever. Their deep connection on stage had been unmistakable. "Maybe we'll see you then."

"Six weeks," it sounded so long. "Nowhere sooner?"

"We'll be at sea on the Vic-Maui Return for the next five weeks. The only place we'll be playing is on the sailboat."

It had been impossible to miss the mayhem that had hit Lahaina. A banner year, twenty-three yachts had completed the long race. Two more were still expected, after the time limit had expired but in time for tonight's party. Three more had retired and dropped out. Several hundred sailing crew had hit the small town of Lahaina as if they'd been at sea for two years not two weeks.

"You're sailing back to Victoria for five weeks?" Vonda couldn't imagine what that would be like.

"Sure. We've done it several times."

And it was one of *those* moments.

Vonda felt herself rising up on her toes as if to resist falling forward from a gentle nudge behind. Taking the next step after Greg had walked out on her. Getting on the plane to Hawaii. Going...

One of those moments she'd so often dodged in the past.

The past.

Done with wallowing, huh?

She opened her eyes and looked at the woman.

Vonda still didn't know her name.

It didn't matter.

The wind was blowing from behind her. She'd sailed before. Never on one of the big boats like the line of forty- and fifty-footers presently anchored off Lahaina's shore. But she'd sailed. That had to count for something, didn't it?

"Need another hand? I've sailed in smaller boats."

"It's four or five weeks. And there can be some bad storms."

"Don't care." Even if there was no music, no dancing. "If there's no room on yours, how about another boat? How do I find out? I mean—"

The woman's smile cut her off.

Vonda bit her tongue and tried to chill. Something she'd never been particularly good at...before the cancer. It was actually kind of neat that the excitement had come back. Until now she'd wondered if she'd ever be excited about something again.

"I'll ask around. Meet us for breakfast tomorrow at seven in the 808 Grindz Cafe?"

"Sure. I like that place." She'd actually eaten her way through most of the menu and put on some much-needed weight as she'd inhaled a three-egg omelet with fried spam, corned beef hash, and ham fried rice on successive mornings. She rarely needed lunch after one of their breakfasts, but the place was addictive.

"Okay, I'd better go catch up with Myles. He'll eventually notice I'm missing. I don't want him thinking I'm dead on the road." And she motored off.

"Thanks!" Vonda thought to shout too little too late. But the woman, whose name she still didn't know, raised a hand in a wave and raced out of the parking lot. At least raced as fast as an island scooter could go.

Vonda repeated Myles' name a few time to be sure to remember it.

"Well now you've done it, Vonda," she said to no one at all.

She had.

"No commitments needed until you step on the boat."

Too late. She was so there already.

5

———————

Seven a.m. at the 808 Grindz?

Vonda was there at six with her backpack beside her. By six-thirty she'd turned a Mowie Wowie omelet into a thousand tiny egg cubes on her plate, her hot cocoa was cold, and her pineapple juice warm.

At six-fifty, a big guy in his fifties came in, and scanned the diners. His eyes locked on her and he headed straight over to her sitting alone at a table for four.

Oh shit!

She checked around. The place was busy enough that he wouldn't try anything here. But she'd have to leave to get away from him. Then he might follow. And Vonda would miss the musicians. And—

"You the one wants to sail the return?"

The relief and disappointment warred within her. He wasn't a threat, but it meant she'd be on a different boat than the musicians. Vonda managed a weak nod.

He sat down across from her without asking. Would she feel safe on this guy's boat? What if it was just them? She didn't like the sound of that at all.

"Why should I let you on my boat?" He flagged down a waitress for a cup of coffee.

His arrogance ticked her off. He reminded him too much of her fiancé…ex-fiancé. "Why should *I* want to go on *your* boat? Plenty to choose from."

His smile was fast. "Most of the crews are already set. You're running out of choices."

Crap! She'd barely slept throughout the night, instead imaging sailing out of the past she'd been mired in. And now the life had gone out of it.

"Are you spooking my new friend, Barry?" The musician woman slid into one of the open seats.

"Nah, Rose. Just trying to find out if she's a good one or if you'll have to dump her overboard after the first hundred miles."

Vonda couldn't suppress the squeak of fear that being set adrift in the middle of the ocean evoked.

"Your sense of humor is one of the reasons we're glad you're flying home this afternoon." Rose said in her quiet steady way.

Breathe, Vonda reminded herself. *Just breathe.*

Barry rolled his eyes. "Just having a bit of fun. Seriously though," he didn't look any more or less serious as he turned back to face Vonda, "what *are* your qualifications?"

Vonda tried to come up with some, but couldn't. "Absolutely none. The biggest boat I've ever been on was a Cal 23, cruising on Lake Washington."

"Cruising? More like wallowing on a fat rubber ducky in a bathtub! Long damn way from my J/160." Barry looked aside, "This is the one you want to take deep sea, Rose?"

Vonda quickly repeated Rose a few times. Myles and Rose. Myles and Rose.

Rose shrugged. "She asked. I like her."

Barry looked back and forth between them, then finally nodded. "Your call. There's enough foul weather gear aboard to take care of her. The return isn't my ride, just my boat. So don't break her on the way home." He slugged back the rest of his still-steaming coffee like it was a shot of tequila, pushed back, and tipped his head toward Vonda. "Might be nice for my liability insurance if you don't break the girl either."

A silence settled over the table after he was gone. Rose waited long enough for the jumble of Vonda's thoughts to settle.

"Me? You like me? But you don't know me." Not that she knew Myles or Rose either.

"Do I need a reason?" Rose's smile was easy to return.

"Not if it gets me on the boat."

6

———

Her afternoons on Margo's Cal 23 puttering around Lake Washington did nothing at all to prepare her for the *Maybelline*. Six people could fit in the cockpit of Margo's little twenty-three-footer, hip-to-shoulder and bumping knees.

The *Maybelline* was an awe-inspiring fifty-three feet long and fifteen wide. The mast towered forever above her head. The cockpit was filled with a bewildering array of lines, winches, and a steering wheel so big that there was a notch in the deck for the lower part to swing in. But eight could still sit on the cushioned seats, not counting the person behind the wheel.

"How many people are needed to sail it?" she asked Rose.

"To sail *her?* Two can manage for a cruise. On the race down, she had a crew of ten. Helmsman, navigator, two winchmen, and a foredeck hand. Two watches."

Vonda's unintended glance at her bare wrist earned Rose's soft laugh. Vonda knew what it meant and struggled not to feel foolish as Rose explained.

"A watch is a shift. But on a boat like this that's a loose term. One of us can handle the boat in most conditions, two if it gets nasty. All ten if you're racing hot in a strong blow, whether or not it's your time to sleep."

"There are going to be ten of us?" It was a big boat, but that would be a bigger crowd than she'd hung out with in a long time.

"Three. You're the third. We'll up-anchor as soon as Myles gets here with the rest of the groceries." Myles, Myles, she repeated a few more times. His name had become a mantra of hope somewhere in the long night. Myles and Rose.

Vonda hadn't thought about the food. Five weeks' worth for her to be aboard. "I can pay for—"

Rose waved it away. "Barry pays for it. It's traditional. Most boat return crews are unpaid, but the owner covers all expenses to have his boat sailed home. You get the forward cabin. Go ahead and stow your gear. I'll scrounge slicks, a float jacket, and a life preserver for you before we go."

"Like a kid?"

"Underway, we'll all wear them except in the calmest weather *and* we're all three awake. You'll get used to it." Rose waved her below.

Vonda descended the ladder into the main cabin and could only gawk.

Margo's Cal 23 had two tiny bunks that were buried under rubber bumpers used at dock, a scattering of lines, and a cooler of beer squashed in among the raincoats.

The *Maybelline* was finished throughout in lustrous wood planking like...she didn't know what...a sailboat? To her left was an efficient kitchen that would be perfect for a luxury studio apartment. A top-opening fridge and freezer were set into the countertop. It had a sink, lots of cupboards, even a small stove and oven. It swung lightly back and forth with the rocking of the boat. She gave it a poke and it swung more. Oh, for when the boat was heeled over, it would stay level. Neat!

To her right was a seat with a table surrounded by more radios and navigation gear than she'd ever imagined. The table was like those old school desks with the lift-up lid. She peeked and it held logbooks and charts, presumably if the equipment broke down. In a drawer she found a steel sextant. That made her feel a little safer, though she had no idea how to use one. An instruction book was tucked in beside it and Vonda vowed to learn that skill before they reached Seattle.

As she moved forward, there were big comfortable bench seats to either side, long enough to stretch out on, and a folded-up table in the middle of the aisle. With the flaps raised, it could seat at least six or seven comfortably.

Beyond that was a grand master suite—at least grand in a very small-space way. A bed big enough for two on the left. Closet and dresser on the right. Straight ahead a shower and sink, and a toilet with enough levers to run a spaceship. She'd definitely need lessons on that. There was a big round metal pole by the door that she finally realized was the bottom of the mast that passed through the floor as well.

But this couldn't be right. Rose and Myles must sleep here, yet there were no clothes or personal stuff.

She set her pack down on the deck and returned aft to ask what she was missing.

As she returned, she saw what it was for herself.

Because she'd been facing forward, she'd missed that to either side of the ladder descending from the cockpit, toward the rear, were two more suites. Each had a bed as big as the one up forward. Oddly, there was gear stowed in both of those rather than all in one.

She also found a second bathroom behind a closed door. Well, maybe the forward suite actually was hers, far more luxury than she'd expected. Vonda had imagined a bigger version of Margo's plastic-coated bench seats in a cramped cabin.

This boat she could happily move aboard and never leave.

"Here, catch!" A male voice called. She turned barely in time to catch a bag with three big loaves of fresh-baked bread.

That was how she met Myles Lauer.

7

____

"Are we racing?" Vonda asked in breathy excitement.

Somewhere around the time they graduated from cradles to cribs, Myles had learned to trust Rose's judgement of people. So, he wasn't worried about Vonda Decosta, but he didn't know quite what to make of her either.

She was cute, pleasant, and her arms and legs were about as big around as pencils. But a joy radiated from the woman that made the sun shine brighter off the tropical water and the greens of Maui hillsides beckon deeper and richer.

He always spent too much time worrying, and Vonda brought none of that. She appeared to be a carefree sprite on the verge of hyperventilating with her passion. And she was being damned cute in the process.

"Not real racing," Rose answered before he could. "A lot of the return boats depart at the same time. Think of it as a casual race but mostly it's safety in numbers if anyone gets in trouble. We'll spread out over time, but probably never more than a day or so apart. Though we could well be in the lead most of the way, *Maybelline* is the largest and one of the fastest boats this year."

Myles tried to remember the last time Rose had said as many words in a row. He couldn't.

As he had the helm at the moment, Rose led Vonda around the boat, preparing for departure. They were anchored offshore in the Lahaina Roads, but the boat had been wrapped up tight during the week since its arrival.

Rose demonstrated how to prep the lines and then the two of them began unwrapping the sails. When they were ready, he raised the main and heaved it in close. That kept *Maybelline's* bow into the wind.

Then they set the big forward genoa, but left it to slap in the breeze.

Rose made quick work of heaving the anchor aboard, securing it, and making sure all of the rode, both chain and line, were fed cleanly into the chain locker.

He could see that Vonda was game, but she was even weaker than her thin limbs made her look. Oh well, she could still help with chores and cooking. Keep a soul company on those long silent watches.

At least she wasn't a chatterer.

While they secured the anchor, he spun the wheel to starboard. *Maybelline* drifted backward and twisted as she came off the anchor and the sails took the wind. They lost less than a boat length before there were moving forward. He spun the wheel to center, hauled in on the gennie sheet, and they were eased ahead smoothly.

A casual glance around showed he wasn't first off the anchor...but he was close. And because the others were to the south, he was first on the northern tack up the Roads, the channel between Maui and Molokai.

He didn't much care, but Barry had been at the dock to

see him off. *Give 'em hell, Myles.* He'd bet that Barry was watching from the shore and grinning as they pulled away first. The man was competitive in ways Myles would never understand.

His body remembered as much as he did himself. As the sails drew, the boat began to put on way, he was already coiling lines properly to set for the next tack—though with these perfect winds, that could be hundreds of miles ahead.

As he worked in the cockpit while Rose and Vonda finished on the deck, he felt the music of the waves wash over him. It had been far too long since he'd sailed. Barry had missed last year's race with a fractured keel, and it had been too late to arrange a ride with anyone else.

Once they were cleaned up and solidly underway, he made a strumming motion to signal Rose to grab his guitar. *Maybelline* had settled into her course like a prime mare out for a lazy canter, loping over the waves with little tending needed. He set the autopilot and watched for a minute to make sure it was behaving.

He took the small travel guitar, plugged in a book-sized powered-speaker, and gave it a strum to check the tuning as he rested a foot on one of the lower wheel spokes so that he could keep track of what the autopilot was up to.

Myles fooled around with a few minor chords, but it wasn't a minor chord sort of day. C? No, the slightly deeper G, they were on an ocean, not a lake.

Vonda dropped an iced tea in the holder by the wheel for him, and then stretched out on a cockpit seat as if she'd never been anywhere else. That smile of purest joy was plastered on her face.

He futzed around with a few chords, but decided to keep it simple. It was that sort of a ride on the waves today.

"*Sailing it's...*" he started out then spotted the look of bliss on Vonda's face, "*Such a joy.*" He tried the line a few times with different cord progressions. Nope, keep it simple: G, C.

"*Sailing it's such a joy...*" he repeated it a few times. First with a folk strum, then he tried picking some of the notes, and finally settled on an upbeat sea chanty strum.

"*Sailing it's such a joy.*" The autopilot briefly lifted, then lowered his foot on the wheel spoke. Like he was playing in a bathtub. "*Sailboat just a big kid's toy.*" Barry was definitely a big kid when it came to the subject of his sailboat.

Myles tweaked the autopilot heading as they cleared the Lahaina Roads and headed north into the open sea. Rose ran out the main and gennie for best draw on the new heading.

"*Sailing along that reach,*" a glance behind, "*Anchor right off the big gold beach.*"

He backtracked through the two lines as Rose brought out her bass and a small speaker of her own. He was running G, C, D, G...but that felt like a verse, not a chorus.

Rose thumped out a G, C, G, D. Rocking the chords with the rhythm of the boat. Absolutely right.

> *Sippin' wine with the settin' sun,*
> *Stars coming out, look I see first one!*
> (He always loved the first night at sea.)
> *Sailing's just right for me.*
> *I'm just a natural born sailor, can't you see!*

He rocked the melody back and forth a few times as Rose came in under him to set it solid and ocean deep.

A verse. Hmm... He eyed Vonda. Clearly a neophyte.

> *First time I ever sailed a boat,*
> *Could hardly believe I was afloat,*

Sailed upon a little lake,
(Rose had told him about her sole experience on Lake
Washington.)
Oops! Watch that sail, feel the sun bake.
Was a time of so much joy,
Back when I was jes' a little-bitty (girl didn't fit, so he put in
himself) *boy.*

All morning they fooled with verses. He sang a sailor's lifetime of verses. Spinning out different versions until they merged and blurred.

When finally his fingers were sore and his stomach was growling, he put aside the guitar.

"Damn I wish I'd recorded some of that."

Vonda handed him a notebook and a pen with a well-chewed end.

And there it was.

Three verses and a tight chorus. The first verse hadn't changed much, all about the joy of sailing. The second verse of adventures. Good lines that Vonda had mixed and matched. He'd never put them together this way, but there the adventures were: dolphins off the bow, the small port towns, and the new friends that always floated there.

The third verse was years later. Not some romantic ending, which he typically shied away from. Nor old age looking back, one of his most common endings. It was still wrapped up in the joy of living:

I sailed some years upon the seven seas,
One fine day while reachin' on a breeze.
Saw something big way up ahead, (dramatic pause)
School o' whales just a-gettin' out of bed.

The last couplet didn't work, nor could he find one he liked in the three pages of notes and scratchings. But when he played it through, the full circle came out and had Vonda scrabbling to take the notebook back and write it down.

They seemed so free and full of joy,
Reminded me of that little-bitty boy!

Full circle. It wasn't big, deep, or important. It was pure fluff, but rife with emotion, the emotion of joy from a life spent sailing.

He looked up at Vonda, "You're hired."

Her smile was radiant.

8

———————

Vonda felt as if she'd been drugged with far more than a turkey sandwich on fresh-baked sourdough and too much sugar in her iced tea.

She hadn't dared sing along, of course.

Couldn't believe she'd handed over the verses at all. But she hadn't been thinking as she'd scribed and rearranged what Myles had spilled out so effortlessly. Then he'd asked for his own words so she'd handed her notes over before she could stop herself.

It was like Woodie Guthrie, one of the greatest folk singers of all time. He'd spent his entire life spinning out tunes. Hundreds had been collected, but thousands more had probably been played once and lost in the winds atop a train or in front of a campfire as he hoboed around the country for so much of his life. They might *all* have been lost if Alan Lomax hadn't discovered him and recorded so many of them.

Myles would have been willing to let his words spill out over the ocean and be lost.

Yet he'd so captured how she was feeling.

Last night, when she'd called home, Mom had been all worried. Dad had simply said, *Sounds like fun, honey. Do it.*

And here she was on the first day of her first big sailing adventure—and there was a song about it. That was crazy, wild, and wonderful.

The next few days were wet, not stormy, but the rain was steady enough that there was no music on deck.

Rose and Myles had slowly trained her to handle the big wheel, and then the sails. The autopilot did the work most of the time, but they turned it off to teach her. Even with the autopilot, she never stood a watch alone, but she was helping.

Not *being* helped, instead helping.

And the power of steering the big boat was a visceral thrill as if her heart had come alive for the first time in a year.

"You're getting the hang of it," Rose said. It was the six-to-midnight watch. The rain had been left behind and the first stars were peeking through holes in the clouds, seeing if it was safe to come out.

"Thanks." Vonda could be casual around Rose. Myles was still up on a pedestal: musical, funny, handsome, and kind. All except one thing, "Can I ask a personal question?"

And there it lay like a dead fish on the deck with no way for her to pretend she wasn't the one who'd tossed it there.

Rose shrugged a yes, only visible in the darkness because of the phosphorescent wake their passagewas churning up in the ocean.

"Don't you two get along? I mean you're not breaking up, are you?" It came out as a whisper in the night. She could feel Myles sleeping in his bed directly below where they both sat in the cockpit, only feet away.

She could feel Rose's attention but couldn't see her expression or read her silence.

"I mean, you looked so close when I saw you play that night. And you look like an incredible couple from the outside. But you sleep apart. I haven't even seen you touch except to steady each other. I—" Vonda finally managed to get control of her mouth. But it was so wrong.

It's not what she'd been dreaming of when she'd gotten engaged to Greg. It was what she'd feared would never be for her as she lost hair, energy, and the will to do more than survive.

Rose let the night be her answer for a long time before speaking. "Twins."

"What about twins?"

"Us. Myles and me. We're twins. Eleven minutes apart."

Vonda wondered if Rose could see how wide her eyes were. "You... But... No, I saw you two play together. How you were together. How..."

Again, Rose's silence seemed to fill the night for a long while before she spoke. "We've always been really close, twins after all. Whole family is. The music maybe makes that closer because we both love it so much. And when we perform, we've found it useful to let people think we're a couple. Keeps the assertive groupies at bay. We used to play the field after each gig, but that gets old fast. Better to let folks assume whatever it is they want to assume while we're on stage. Off stage, out of sight, is when we each find someone to be with."

"And have you found somebody?"

"No." Vonda could hear the wistful sadness. And much later, when Vonda was almost asleep in her seat, lulled by the roll of the waves and the soft green glow fading behind them, "Neither has Myles."

9

———

Myles hadn't woken the girls for the six-a.m. changeover because the sunrise had been too lovely to miss. At the nine-a.m. radio check-in, the next nearest boat was six hours and forty miles behind. *Maybelline* was riding the big rollers of the North Pacific like the champion she was. The autopilot had it down. The nights were growing cooler, it wouldn't be shorts and t-shirt at night much longer.

He tiptoed down to fetch his guitar and plugged in a set of headphones. Because he was fingerpicking, the strings were quieter than the creak of the sails. He wouldn't disturb anyone.

Playing through the sailing song, it was impossible not to smile at the morning because it was such a cheery tune. Something was missing, though he wasn't sure quite what. It wasn't Rose's bass line and her rich alto harmony; he could hear those as clearly in his head as if it was his own voice. There was...something more. But try as he could, it eluded him.

Do something else and maybe it would come to him.

He fooled around with some chords, found a pleasant

rhythm. It was more ballad and less dance. Their money was in the dance music, but out here in the middle of the ocean, who cared.

> *You never believe it could happen to you,*
> *I don't believe it could happen to me.*
> *Just got together, can't you see?*
> *Two of us just walking along.*

Again the chords were ridiculously simple, but they fit the song.

He tinkered together a couple of verses, but it was the refrain that kept shifting. Not that the first chorus was wrong, but that the chorus evolved, revealing the emotions, as the verses told the surface story. The changing refrain that he'd discovered with the mystery dancer at The Dirty Monkey.

> *Two of us just sailing along.*
> (as the ride smoothed out)
>
> ...
>
> *Two of us just livin' along.*
> (as a relationship became a life)
>
> ...
>
> *Two of us just lovin' along*
> (that clear soprano he'd been missing before sounded clear on the morning air and—)

"Whoa!" He snapped back into the moment, realized he'd been singing aloud, and stared at Vonda sitting across the cockpit from him with her notepad in her hand. "Do that again."

"I—" she blushed fiercely. "Sorry, I didn't mean to." She

clenched the notepad in her fist, dropped her pen, reached for it, left it, and scrambled for the ladder to go below.

"No. Wait!"

"What's up?" Rose was half up the ladder, still blinking with sleep.

Vonda, with her escape blocked, turned at bay.

Myles started the chorus again.

He watched Vonda as she stared down at the deck, her jaw clenched. Her grace and balance were shot. He could see that her knees were locked as tightly as her fists but he didn't understand why.

He tried nudging her pen toward her.

She didn't bend down to reach for it. It rolled back and forth with the boat's motion until it bumped against her toe. *That* jolted her to life as if she'd been electrocuted.

She scooped it up, then stumbled on the next wave and crash landed on one of the cockpit seats. Pushing herself upright, she closed her notepad, fruitlessly trying to flatten out the pages she'd crumpled, but still she didn't sing.

Rose had been nodding her head to the tune. She took a deep breath, and opened her mouth.

Myles stopped her joining in with the least shake of his head, and began to repeat the chorus. Still playing the chords that no one but he could hear.

Without looking up, Vonda joined in the second line so softly that it was a whisper barely louder than the wind. By the third line, he could hear her clearly, by the last she was up to perhaps half the volume it should be sung.

It didn't matter. She didn't offer some high harmony. Nor did she echo his melody. As if she too could hear where Rose's voice and bass would slide in seamlessly, she left everything else behind and stitched the two together into a whole.

A countermelody? More of a riff that wandered so far away from the core that it almost sounded wrong until it came back twice as strong when it rejoined his melodic line.

He tried running the refrain again, but this time she kept her silence without looking up.

The chords came to a jangling end over his headphone.

"What did you—"

"Myles," Rose cut him off as she came out on deck. "Why don't you make us some breakfast?"

"But she," he pointed to Vonda though he didn't know *but she* what.

Rose gave him her stop-being-an-idiot eyebrow raise.

Not knowing what else to do, he headed below.

10

This morning Vonda felt none of the peace of sitting in the cockpit with Rose that had so filled last night. She wore cutoffs and a loose shirt that hid her shape and kept the bulk of the sun off her fair skin. SPF50 took care of the rest. But it didn't block all of the nerves inside.

She could feel Rose waiting for her to speak first. As if Vonda had any idea what to say. Maybe tossing herself over the side *wasn't* the worst option.

What was the harm in singing? Yet she'd sung with professional musicians who were completely out of her league. And to take Myles' music and play with it? *Change* it. Yet he hadn't been upset. Instead she'd had the closest thing to a panic attack since...she was twelve?

"I'm the most ridiculous person on the planet!"

Rose did her quiet thing a while longer before asking, "When was the last time you sang?"

"About five minutes ago. Last time *ever!*"

"Um-hmm." Rose did something with the mainsail that Vonda was fairly sure was wholly unnecessary.

"Forever ago. College *a cappella.*" Vonda had enjoyed

that. Unaccompanied singing in a group required immaculate tone and immense creativity. They'd been good, too. Did a couple of intercollegiate competitions and ended up near the top.

Rose re-coiled the line she'd displaced but didn't look up as she spoke. "You know that Myles spent three straight days looking for you. Of course, he still hasn't figured out it was you."

"He did? Wait! That *what* was me?"

"I think you're a *who* not a *what* but I'm just guessing."

"Rose!"

Rose finally looked at her and smiled. She'd burned away Vonda's nerves by ticking her off.

"That *who* was me?"

Through the hatch from below Myles began handing out breakfast: mugs of coffee in steel to-go cups, orange juice in sippy bottles that wouldn't spill, and bowls of yogurt with Grape Nuts, fresh fruit, and a drizzle of honey. All that healthy fiber she was supposed to eat regularly and so rarely did.

He finally joined them.

Rose was keeping a half smile to herself—mostly. Vonda was slowly learning that Rose might be quiet, but she was sneaky. Myles reminded her of the golden retriever they'd had when she was a kid, fun and always eager—but not nearly so deep a thinker.

Vonda concentrated on her breakfast.

"Myles," Rose said so casually that Vonda went on instant alert. Was it too late to go eat in her cabin? "Why don't you tell Vonda about your mystery dancer?"

"Mystery dancer?" And Vonda knew she'd put her foot in it. Now she'd have to stay.

As he began telling the story of their first night at The

Dirty Monkey, Rose's smile grew. Part of it was clearly at some joke Vonda didn't understand, yet. But most of it was love for her brother. She could see that now. Being twins explained so much of the dynamic between them. They were so...

Myles began talking about the mystery dancer—*Mystery Dancer* Rose mouthed at her without interrupting her brother—who had appeared early in the second set.

"Always at the back of the crowd. Hard to see. With this long Hawaiian scarf covering her hair. But my God the way she danced."

The more he explained, the more Vonda suspected.

Her?

It was impossible. Myles wasn't describing her physicality, her out-of-shape body, the betrayal of her breasts producing a cancer that had shattered the life she'd known. He was describing her like...music.

Definitely her.

"I, we," he nodded to include Rose, "have never played like that before. Or since. It was like an ocean I'd never sailed before, and now never can again. I searched for her, but she never came back."

"Are you sure you'd recognize her when she does?" Rose winked at Vonda.

"How could I miss her? An angel of music. She could croak like a frog and still be a muse. She made the music do things I can't find again."

"It's only been a few days."

"Nine days. Nine days and eleven goddamn hours from the end of that last set to now!" It was the first time she'd heard words of anger from either of the twins. He looked at his watch. "And fourteen minutes!" he practically spit it out.

Vonda shook her head.

No! Rose *thought* it had been her but, even if she was right, she was still wrong. It was impossible. Vonda knew she was a broken thing, not some magic talisman that Myles wished to worship from afar.

Vonda collected their empty bowls and carried them below to wash.

She avoided the sadness in both of their eyes: Myles at his loss and Rose at Vonda's cowardice.

11

———

"Are you okay?" Myles kept his voice low.

All yesterday and last night there'd been no sign of Vonda. And Rose hadn't said an unneeded word, which with the unusually fine sailing weather had been few and far between.

Vonda looked...haunted when she emerged into the morning sunlight. He searched her face for the joy that had been there the day she'd boarded the boat, but it had been wiped away.

She shook her head no. "But hiding isn't fixing anything." She eased onto the seat on the other side of the big wheel he sat behind. It was like she was cut up into pieces by the spokes. She looked so upset that he moved from the helmsman's seat to sit across from her in front of the wheel.

The wind was unusually steady, no storm nor any expected. *Maybelline* was managing well on the new heading Rose had tacked to last night. They had altered course from due north to northeast as the North Pacific Gyre turned to join the Japanese current. If this held, they could maybe even fly the spinnaker, though even with three that would be a challenge. Definitely not two with their level of experience.

"Is it something I said?"

Again she shook head, but then she offered an uncertain shrug.

"We can double back. It'll be a rougher ride against the wind, but *Vapor* is only fifteen hours behind us. I'm sure they have room if you want to change boats."

She shook her head again; no follow-up shrug this time.

"Do you want me to get Rose? She's worried about you." Or maybe pissed at him, but when he'd asked, she'd simply said, *Your watch,* then gone below. "I guess I am too."

"I..." Vonda's voice cracked from lack of use, then she swore so violently that he laughed. "I'm so *sick* of being frail."

"Then don't be."

She looked up at him. Her light brown eyes studying his face. "It's not that easy."

"Sure it is. There's the past, the present, and the future. Which do you want to live in?"

"Myles," it was the first time she'd used his name and he liked the way it sounded. "The past has consequences."

"Does it?"

When she started to protest, he rested a hand on hers to stop her. It was the first time they'd touched. Her hands weren't frail, they were delicate.

"I'm not being facetious. So many great songwriters have covered this ground. Kathy Matea, *You've Got to Dance.*"

"Yeah, sure. Tim McGraw, *Live Like You Were Dying.* Been there. Done that." She looked even sadder which shouldn't be possible.

He wanted to grab his guitar and play a song for her but

a tune about the joys of sailing didn't seem on the mark at the moment. He knew his own shortcomings.

"Look, Vonda, I'm crap at expressing myself except through music. Half the time I don't even hear..." And then her words sunk in.

"*Been there? Done that?*"

She seemed to cower, but nodded.

"Are you okay now?"

"Except for the lifetime threat of relapse, *sure.*" Then she slapped her hand across her mouth and almost darted down the ladder once more.

He kept his hand on hers to keep her in place. "I can't imagine how hard that must be."

"It's..." her voice choked behind her hand, "...not easy."

Unsure what else to do, he shifted to sit beside her and went to pat her on the back. Surprisingly, she turned into his shoulder and burst into tears.

It only took seconds before Rose was halfway up the ladder and glaring at him.

What's happening, he mouthed to her.

Rose froze in position, listening to Vonda's weeping, then nodded to herself. She descended the stairs again and he heard her room's door close. That was crazy.

Unable to move, he stroked Vonda's short hair, fluffy and softer than any he'd ever touched before. Then he ran his hand down her back in what he hoped was a soothing gesture.

For a mile or more, the only sound on board was the slap of lines and Vonda's quiet sniffles. He looked for something to distract himself from how nice she felt in his arms. Sun was up in the sky. A few clouds too small to portend anything, just going about their own business. The rollers wide and deep rocked the boat gently. Not a bird around. He didn't see them much this far out, unless there was a big school of fish for them to feast on. He could even hear the tiny hum of the autopilot as its motors whirred on and off to maintain their heading.

Finally Vonda sniffled to herself and apologized quietly.

"No problem. I'm always at a loss about what to do with a weeping woman. This is nothing new."

"A lot of practice?" she managed on a choked voice.

"Not a lot, but some."

She patted his shoulder. "You do just fine, Myles."

"Something you want to talk about?"

Vonda shook her head. "But I guess you earned the right to know."

His emotions went through a thousand changes as she told him the story of her illness. Shock, pity, blind fury at her asshole fiancé's dumping her, and all the rest of it.

"And you call yourself frail? I hope I'm half as strong if anything like that ever comes my way. You are sailing thousands of miles across the open ocean. You know how few people would dare do that, never mind actually try? Right there, you're a rare breed."

"You aren't repulsed?"

"Why would I be?"

Vonda studied him from so close he could see the patterns of her irises. "Or pitying me?"

"Feeling sorry for you, sure. That was a rough storm to ride through. But it makes me think more rather than less of you for coming through that with so much joy."

"Joy?" she gasped in disbelief.

He sang,

First time I ever sailed a boat...

She threw her head back and laughed like a release. She joined him on the chorus. Somewhere in the second verse, Rose came on deck with their bass and guitar and soon the three of them were singing together.

They repeated the chorus several times, each building on the one before. Vonda's voice soon soared above theirs in flights of purest fancy.

And his fingers shifted. Not changing the chords, but augmenting them. Adding notes from his low E-string when Rose climbed up from her bass' high-G. Finding flourishes to tease Vonda's high notes that sent her spinning off into—

His fingers jangled on the strings.

"Holy shit!" He turned to Vonda. "I've been looking everywhere for you!"

Vonda cringed. She'd forgotten herself and let Myles' kindness sweep her away. It had felt so good to let the music unleash all of the pain she hadn't been able to show in front of her parents. A year's pain and fear had spilled out of her —and turned to joy.

That was the miracle.

That, and Myles hadn't walked away.

Instead, he'd held her hand and told her how amazingly strong she was.

That wasn't any version of herself she recognized.

Myles turned to Rose but pointed his finger at Vonda, "She'd MD." Then he turned to face her. "You're MD."

"No, I'm V, Vonda Decosta."

"No you aren't. You're the woman who made the music with her body. Seriously, I spent three straight days driving Rose crazy as I combed Lahaina looking for you."

"And now that you found me?" She held up her chin. She wasn't merely some phantom.

He'd driven her to go and hide in her cabin because he'd painted a picture of a living miracle that she could never live up to. She'd had Myles on a pedestal, still did. But he'd had her standing atop a skyscraper.

And yet...he didn't.

She'd lost her shit and spilled her life all over the cockpit.

His response was fury at Greg—and telling her how amazing she was.

"Now that I found you?" Myles laughed. "First, you're going to get out that damn notebook of yours."

"And then?"

He kissed her on the nose. "And then, who knows!"

13

Vonda stood on the edge of the stage at Q Nightclub. The place was packed. She managed a wave to Mom and Dad, seated on the edge of the dance floor but not for long. She knew Mom would drag Dad onto the floor soon enough.

Three months after coming ashore to work on their act and attract the attention of the bigger clubs. What would three more months bring?

"Tonight, at the Q," an announcer called out, "we're proud to present VMR, the Vic-Maui Return Band."

The three of them had agreed that the band's name had two meanings. The public one and the private one just for them: Vonda, Myles, and Rose.

Rose lay down a heavy bass beat that caught everyone's attention. It was the irresistible pulse of the sea. Sure enough, Mom was already rising to her feet.

Vonda felt her knee flex with the rhythm to keep her balance, as would be necessary on a sailboat slipping over the waves.

Myles slid in with a happy pulse of dolphins.

The beat was building through her body as Myles and Rose built the ocean through which the song would swim.

The crowd was shifting from the bar and tables to the dance floor. Soon the place was hopping.

Vonda felt the full song.

She felt the music they'd built during their four remaining weeks on the sea. The beauty of starry skies and brilliant sunrises. The agony of fear turned to ecstasy by the first time she and Myles had made love. They'd skipped over dating and sex and moved straight into the purest joy she'd ever found.

She glanced at Rose so lost in the music that her eyes had slid shut.

Maybe they'd find a fourth initial someday. Someone for her future sister-in-law.

For now, Vonda gave herself to the music.

Her eyes were wide open. She saw the journey so clearly. Not the one downwards that had come so close to finishing her. Her imagination and her heart were caught in the upwards one ahead that was so rich with promise.

She'd have to suggest the idea to Myles, he was their master composer. He built, Rose embellished, and Vonda brought the wind to fill the sails.

She lifted her mike to her mouth and let the joy race ahead.

NARROWBOAT GODDESS

ABOUT THIS STORY

Alice paints narrowboats that cruise the UK canals. Her reputation shines as sterling as her art. But when her mentor retires and leaves the company to her, she becomes paralyzed by the task.

Carl simply brought in his parents' boat for a new paint job. But nothing prepares him for the life changes wrought when he meets the artist.

How can they possibly make two uncertain tomorrows, and hearts, merge like two rivers on the canal?

1

―――――

"You're *what?*" Alice felt torn in two.

One moment she'd been deeply immersed in painting a very tricky letter S. The owner of this narrowboat had wanted ornate rather than more traditional lettering. *Samson's Strength*, with its four strong S's, was a name he was immensely proud of. It was also a choice that still befuddled her. John Samson was as bald as a cue ball, so his boat's name said he'd already lost his mythical strength. Her attempts to delicately point this out had only led to mutual confusion when he asked who Delilah was and what she had to do with his boat's name. Alice had desisted.

"I'm retiring." Vincent repeated. "It's the first of April, but this is no Fool's Day joke."

Too abruptly, she'd now been rammed into this new moment, making her head spin. It was a change she couldn't reconcile at all with her artistic headspace. She'd been in the flow, her paintbrush soaring with the pinnacles of a Bach organ Cantata through her earbuds. Bach and Handel were best for lettering work. Mozart and Beethoven were acceptable. After that period, the romantics took over with their over-orchestration and excessive flourishes. They were all *after* the peak of the golden age of canal boating, making them feel too anachronistic when she was working.

"You can't retire." She looked at Vincent, half through her fall of blonde hair and half in the clear. Alice had learned the hard way to never touch her hair while painting, the colors went from hand to hair instantly, no matter how sure she was that her hands were clean. And the one time she used turps, her hair didn't behave or smell right for days.

"Try me. June First, the wife and I are taking that quest I always talked about."

"Boating every mile of the United Kingdom's canals?" He'd talked about it ever since she'd been a little girl, but she'd never thought he'd actually do it. There were over four thousand miles of them. At a canal boat's speed of four miles an hour that would take some time.

"And then we're off to the French canals. After a lifetime of fixing up canal boats, it's time I enjoyed traveling in one."

"But...I don't understand."

His puzzled look had her opening her mouth and then closing it when she couldn't think of how to explain herself. Vincent was more than a mere fixture in her professional life.

She tried again. "I was born here."

He nodded his grey head and smiled. When had Vincent's hair gone grey? She'd never really noticed it before. Sure, she'd incorporated first the shifting grey and later what she thought of as his *distinguished silver* into her color palette but it was still a surprise to fully register it atop his head. They'd celebrated his seventieth birthday only last month.

When Mum had been in her late teens and come off a

holiday fling with a narrowboater only to find herself alone and pregnant, Vincent had taken her in. Alice herself had been born in the narrowboat docked alongside Vincent's shop: K&A Lion, Boat Painters. *You just popped out of the rabbit hole, honey, quick as a bunny. That's why I named you Alice. No time to rush off anywhere. No need either. You and me? We did just fine.*

Mum had never had the knack for working on narrowboats. Instead she'd worked for Vincent's wife Edda in the attached K&A Lion, Pub until Alice was grown. Then she'd had a fling with an American on a narrowboat holiday, married, and now had a second family in Austin, Texas.

"Retiring? But who will run K&A Painters?"

Vincent's smile went radiant. "You will!"

Alice wondered what rabbit hole she'd fallen down. It was mid-morning. The sun shone from above. Two boats rested quietly in the shop's painting slips, waiting to be tended to. But nothing was connecting properly. She could only stare at him in disbelief.

"You've always had it in you. You did your first signboard at age eight. By twelve you'd done your first boat stem to stern. Who else would I possibly sell it to?"

"But," Alice waved her paintbrush and nearly splattered the S in *Strength,* which would be very annoying. She'd already had to take it out once because the curves were all wrong. S's were easier to remove entirely and then retry; attempts to fix them as-is never came out right. "But I can't afford to buy a business."

Vincent appeared to be enjoying her complete discomfiture, "You haven't asked me the price."

"I'm not going to." She set her brush down firmly on her palette, a twelve-hole muffin tin caked thick with a hundred dried colors and currently filled with the four active ones. And in doing so, she polluted her brush with a splash of yellow that was for the boat name's *glow of strength* effect, not the lettering itself. She might have to redo the entire name now if she couldn't exactly match the *virile-red* that John Samson had chosen.

"Ten quid."

She eyed Vincent. He was still offering that annoying smile, but he didn't appear to be joking.

"Oh, give over, Alice. Who else would I ever leave it to? Our boy is gone. You're as close as we ever had to a daughter. Edda was always careful with the coin and has sold the pub for a small fortune, far more than we'll ever need to keep us afloat. We don't need the money. Besides, what else would you possibly do? You were meant for this."

2

She was meant for this?

It had been two weeks since he'd told her, and her throat still constricted too much for her breath to escape.

It had taken Alice four tries to create the final S in *Samson's Strength* and she still wasn't thrilled by it. The owner had been ecstatic, so she'd kept her doubts to herself as he wrote the generous check with a nice tip and motored out onto the Kennet and Avon Canal to show off his fresh-painted narrowboat.

She surveyed the small dockyard that was K&A Lion, Boat Painters. It was her whole world. The double wide shed roof covered two slips for a pair of narrowboats. Seven feet wide and up to seventy long, they had originally carried coal, grain, and passengers from Bristol port and through Bath. From there they'd continued upward along the Avon River, the K&A Canal—where they passed this shop at the top of the Devizes locks, the top of the whole system—and then down the Kennet and Thames Rivers to London at the far end. The same route had carried wealthy Londoners this direction to the social whirl and thermal waters of Bath.

Starting in the mid-1800s, the trains had nearly wiped out the canals. But ambitious volunteers, followed by a great deal of tourism, had brought them back since the 1960s. And Vincent had started K&A Lion, Boat Painters here in Devizes fresh out of secondary school during that resurgence.

The shed roof kept off the rain, the skylights and open sides let in the sun and a gentle wind. The docks were very low to the water to properly paint the freeboard's sides. Redoing the bottom paint in a drydock was left to the repair yards to tackle; K&A was only about the upperworks. Vincent had cobbled together a way to gather the sanding dust so that none drifted onto the other boat, if there were two in the shed, or into the canal waters.

There wasn't an inch of this place that she didn't know— but she'd never wanted to *own* it.

Vincent dealt with the business. With the prices and payments. The schedules. The customers, my word—the customers! All she did was paint the intricate and ever-changing designs on narrowboats.

Nearly all boats bore a large panel on either side, near the stern. Three feet high and six-to-eight long, this was where most of the boat artist's effort typically landed. The boat name, owner, port-of-call, and the builder, if it was known for the more historic vessels.

Some owners desired clean lines and a simple look. Others wanted elaborate re-creations of a luxury that had probably never existed traditionally but were now accepted as such. Complex geometrics, lush flower arrangements, and highly stylized lettering. And yet others broke all *classic* bounds with fantastic or modernist designs.

Her boat, that she and Vincent had slowly fixed up over the years, was tied up along the canal side of the boat shed.

Now it served as their best advertisement, easily visible from the canal and adorned with the finest paint job of them all. It bloomed with whimsical flowers, Victorian lettering (she'd listened to a little Chopin while painting those), and all backed by a boat-long glowing sunrise. Mum had named her and the boat on the same day. Not only *Alice's* signboard, but the entire length of the boat abounded with the whimsical characters of *Alice In Wonderland* frolicking among the flowers. The boat depicted the many sights of Wonderland.

Through the years she'd painted everything from block letters to dark wizards creating the signboard name like a flowing incantation.

Her favorites were when the owners dedicated a section of the panel to: *Make something pretty.* She answered with: flowers, castles, prancing horses, woodlands... Woodlands were the best but she loved them all.

It didn't matter to her what they wanted, as long as they were happy. She threw herself into every panel and every boat.

Vincent had trained her and together they'd spent over a decade making K&A Lion, Boat Painters *the* lauded name up and down the canal. It was rare that either slip under the shed roof was empty for more than a day or so and they often had a waiting list.

She stood at the end of the dock, letting the water calm her while she awaited the next arrival. Her favorite duck family clustered nearby with a fresh float of seven downy chicks. Tossing bits of bread, they welcomed her like one of their own.

But *on* her own? Alice had no idea how she was going to go on with her life without Vincent.

3

Carl almost rammed the boat shed as well as the...vision standing at the tip of the finger pier. The century-old Bolinder engine designed to move a narrowboat at four miles-per-hour over dead calm water wasn't exactly a powerhouse when it came to emergency reversing of his twenty-five-ton craft.

Thankfully, the vision was as quick with a boat pole as she was lovely.

She'd been standing at the end of the boat painter's dock, her long blonde hair floating about her in soft ripples that caught the morning sunlight. Sparkles of the sunrise skipping low off the main canal, played across her features, turning her from human to fairy princess. Her white painter's pants were more multi-color paint spatters than fabric—she'd been thoroughly Jackson Pollacked. Her maroon t-shirt with a roaring golden lion and the company name outlined her slim figure. The sunny smile she offered definitely reached those brilliant blue eyes despite his clumsy arrival.

She must think him an utter fool. That he ended up tied

safely in the slip was far more her doing than his. This had been his family's boat since he was a little boy, and he'd been steering it on summer holidays like an old salt since his teens. But suddenly he was handling it like a pathetic gongoozler.

"Hi, sorry about that. I don't know what came over me."

She offered another shot of that radiant smile. "Any docking made without killing people is a good one."

It was easy to join in her laughter over the old saying as they introduced themselves. He shut down the engine in the cockpit as she snugged off the stern line that he'd handed over.

"You didn't send any drawings or photographs, so let's go over what you want on your boat."

"My parents' boat actually." He hung onto the cabin-roof handrail as he clambered out of the cockpit and edged along where the hull met the cabin.

Narrowboats by their very nature had little spare space above or belowdecks. On top of its sixty-six feet, the rear cockpit had a stand-up tiller and a pair of bench seats that made six a friendly crowd. The distant bow had room for two couples to relax and enjoy the sunset with a post-cruising glass of wine.

The rest was a trunk cabin that ran the length of the boat with a narrow six-inch lip to either side. There was just room for his toes and the balls of his feet as he shuffled sideways hanging onto the roof. At the midpoint, he snagged the spring line that he'd flipped up onto the roof when departing his parents' over-winter mooring a half hour ago.

He hopped down onto the dock, secured the midpoint of the line that was tied both fore and aft to keep the boat steady at the dock, then rose.

He was suddenly mere inches from nose-to-nose contact with Alice.

He was surprised enough to stumble back and land against the boat. It was a good thing he *had* secured the spring line first or he might have fallen into the gap between the boat and the dock.

"Uh, sorry. Being clumsy."

She smiled in a way that said something was amusing her. Perhaps she liked buffoons. Not a role he would normally choose. He was more the confidant center-of-the-business-presentation sort.

"I, uh," he shook his head to clear the slight hypnosis that the lovely painter offered by standing calmly before him. She was exactly what he'd expect if Lewis Carroll's Alice had grown tall and graceful. He turned to the boat.

The *Diana* had generous windows down either side past the rear decorative panels. A tiny container garden of herbs and flowers would sit on the roof all summer. But the paint job was showing its age. The block lettering had merely looked tired until he'd seen the boat *Alice* docked out front, then it had looked—

"Alice!" He turned back to look at the lovely blonde.

"Yes?"

He glanced over the *Diana* toward the boat sitting along the canal. They shared a name. "Is that yours? Mum always insisted that we slow down to a crawl each time we passed it. She adores the *Alice*. Absolutely stunning." He was fairly sure he was talking about the boat.

"Thank you. Now, your boat?"

Carl cleared his throat but it did nothing to clear his head. "It's their fortieth wedding anniversary. As a surprise gift, I wanted to get her repainted. The whole length, full decorative work, not just a coat of paint and the signboard name."

"With what?"

He could only shrug. He didn't really know. "I, uh, want it to be beautiful."

Again that musical laugh. "An homage to Princess Diana?"

"Uh, no. Mum and Dad are Oxford professors. She's a specialist in Ancient Greek and Roman literature; he's a leading translator of Middle English. That's how we were able to spend summers on the canals each year," he was babbling. "And that's where I learned to handle a boat, which—I need to shut up now after that last demonstration. *Diana,*" he took a deep breath and tried to focus, "is for the Roman goddess, the Huntress."

If he'd thought Alice had been smiling before, he'd grossly underestimated the meaning of the word. She...glowed.

"You're giving me a whole boat to paint—based on a Roman woodland goddess—in any way I want as long as it's beautiful? The goddess of the hunt?"

It sounded a little stupid that way, but he shrugged a yes.

Her squeal of delight would have sent him stumbling back against the boat again if she hadn't hugged him tightly in her joy. It only lasted an instant but it fired off every nerve ending in his body.

Their contact had been electric. At least for him.

Her reaction, however, was to begin frantically mumbling to herself. "Oh my God— Oops!" she bowed to the boat. "Oh my God*dess*. I need my sketch pad. Oh thank you. Thank you. Thank you." She briefly grabbed his arm with a grip most guys at his London gym would envy, then rushed away still talking to herself, "Not Gregorian chants.

The medievalists were also of the church, but the wrong church. That would be wrong. I'll have to go with Baroque. No! Opera! *Aida. Tosca. Cleopatra.* Strong women. Yes. Yes."

Diana was moored in the inner slip, which lay parallel to the canal. Another boat occupied the outer slip, and her boat was tied up beyond that.

Alice raced to the head of the dock, raced over to the outside dock, and practically sprinted to the *Alice* narrowboat, before disappearing below.

Carl stood there, alone on the dock except for a few ducks asking if he had bread, and wondered what had just hit him. A blonde whirlwind...who wasn't returning. He rose up on his toes to peek over the two intervening boats. Through the window, he could see she was already hunched over a table and making rapid movements that were probably on her sketch pad.

He checked his watch. The lunch meeting in London couldn't wait. Though he stretched his slack time to the limit, she showed no signs of returning.

By the time he left the dock to make the two-hour drive back to the city, it was at a run. For the first time ever, he was about to conduct a business meeting in jeans and a t-shirt.

4

———

The state of the *Diana* was horrid. Prior painters had layered new paint on old. In places it was rubbed to a patina shine, worn quickly thin because of not anticipating where hands would grasp and ropes would rub day after day. In others it was peeling due to failure of the lower layers. She eased away a long strip near the after-cabin door—it wasn't even bonded to the layer beneath. Someone should be shot for not properly texturing the old surface with a good sanding before applying the new coats.

It took her most of two weeks to sand the boat back to bare wood. A belt or disc sander was out of the question, though she was tempted several times. The risk of dinging the underlying wood was too great, and it was beautiful wood. Atypically rich-grained, maybe she would leave it bare as the background. After all, Diana's natural habitat was the forest.

Grinding off so many layers with an orbital sander took forever but it didn't matter, she wanted it to be perfect.

Not only for the boat's owners, but for herself. Half the time was gone until Vincent and Edda...left. It was the only way she could stand to think of it. How could he do this to her? The amount of time she'd already spent stripping off the old paint had used the bulk of the boat's budget. She knew that was wrong, and stubbornly didn't care.

"I've got no business sense. This is going to be a disaster once you leave. Please take it back or sell it to someone else."

Vincent had smiled in that fatherly way of his, patted her shoulder, and turned back to work on the other boat that had come in: a simple roughen, repaint (with a contrasting trimline), and then the signboard.

He'd taken one look at her Huntress sketches and then insisted that he'd do the other boat himself. Over the next several weeks they worked in side-by-side slips. But she rarely saw him, because she rarely looked up from the project of the *Diana*.

Sometimes she'd be sanding along, with the next-finer grit sandpaper, and she'd come upon a bacon butty sandwich wrapped against the dust or a bottle of cold water that he'd left in her way. Alice would wolf it down, an appropriate analogy for Diana the Huntress' boat, and keep going after mumbling a "Thank you" toward Vincent around a full mouth.

When it was done, when not a single joint had one lurking line of the old color, she finally stopped. The silence was deafening after two weeks of work with buzzing of the orbital sander and grind of the rasp. Bare wood at last.

Vincent came up beside her and they stood looking at the bare canvas of the sixty-six-foot-long boat.

"I couldn't have done it as well myself," he whispered softly.

That didn't give her much comfort.

She'd never questioned her skills in painting. It was only in everything else.

5

Carl stared down at his desk trying to figure out what had just happened.

At least it wasn't the Americans, this time. They always had to go in for the kill, it was in their nature. But no, the unanticipated move had come out of Amsterdam.

One moment he'd been leading the acquisition team through the takeover of a very attractive aerospace manufacturer. Within hours of the agreement being finalized and signed, he'd been called into another meeting —during which their entire company had been acquired by the slippery Dutch. The board had negotiated without him, and had only been awaiting the acquisition of the aerospace company before signing.

Now?

He'd been thanked deeply and given a large bonus for the successful acquisition by the old company, then the new one had given him a generous termination package and a swift boot. Fourteen hours ago he'd been on the verge of having everything. And now? At eight p.m. on a lovely May evening, he'd been asked to make sure his office was cleared out before he went home.

Not knowing quite what he was doing, he'd done so: turned in his pass card to security, and driven out of underground parking—a major perk in the heart of London.

Hours later, almost dawn, with little idea of how or even why he'd driven to where he had, he stopped. He recalled the disconnected towns of Brighton, Portsmouth, Stow-on-the-Wold, Winchcombe, and Bath among others. He'd crisscrossed the much of southern England with no real plan or intent except to drive.

Three in the morning. A quiet country lane... Odd place to stop.

Sells Green, he could see the sign in his headlights. The name was familiar, as familiar as an old friend, though he couldn't recall why at the moment.

Why *had* he stopped here?

Looking down at the blinking red light on the dashboard he saw that he wasn't the one who'd stopped—his car had.

Silence.

Out of gas.

He was on a small slope and used it to roll backward and steer onto the verge before pressing the Engine Off button.

Leaving his suit jacket, but picking up the small box that had been the personal items from his desk, he began walking. Up the climbing road, as that was the direction his car had been going.

The country lane climbed above the flat farmland that stretched off into the darkness to either side. The night was full of stars. The smell of mown hay and fresh-turned soil lay thick upon the darkness. The silence eased London into no more than a passing thought's echo in the dead of night.

He shied away from the thought. *London,* even as a word, did not sit comfortably on his thoughts and the night felt too comfortable to think.

After a lazy curve, he stepped out onto a low brick-sided bridge and knew exactly where he was. Here the road arched over the Kennet & Avon Canal in the middle of the rural hamlet of Sells Green. The main thing it was known for by narrowboaters was a set of municipal-provided trash bins at the canal's edge, and a sign pointing the way to the Three Magpies pub, 281 meters from the canal. That precise *one* was a nice touch.

They'd be closed now. It was okay. He wasn't hungry. Or thirsty. Or tired.

Numb? But he wasn't cold. Shocked? But he hadn't been electrocuted. London? But thankfully the word skidded off his thoughts.

He descended from the bridge down onto the canal-side towpath and turned east. That was toward London, but afoot it was safely too far off to think about. The tall Caen Hill and the Devizes Flight of locks added to the comfortable mental barrier. There was definitely a closer destination...though quite what it was he'd have to take on faith. A strange day, indeed. Yet on careful consideration, he decided it was better not to think beyond that to quite *why* it had been strange.

Once horses had trodden here to pull the canal boats. A single horse could easily drag a thirty-ton narrowboat filled with fifty tons of cargo for hours along the dirt way. In modern times the path was paved and had become the kingdom of walkers, cyclists, and families who picnicked down its length.

Tonight, it bore the weight of a lone pedestrian—and no ghosts. At least not any unfriendly ones.

Set down among the trees, the water was as silent as the night. Lights shone off to either side from time to time… There was a sliver of a moon… The water a mirror-smooth companion that looked as if he could walk upon it, though he decided he'd stick with the towpath tonight. Wide and well-paved, it was a sufficient guide.

Some unmeasurable time later, he reached the base of the Devizes Flight. It was officially one of the Seven Wonders of the UK Waterways. Its straight climb up the face of Caen Hill included sixteen consecutive locks that lifted and lowered the boats most of the two-hundred-plus-foot difference between the Avon River behind and the Kennet River ahead.

In the starlight, the long line of lock gates climbing the long hill looked as if some giant had spilled his Meccano set onto the grassy slope.

Nestled in the base of the flight, he could see the outlines of sleeping canal boats tied up along the waterway. Their owners perhaps too exhausted from the five-hour descent to brave the last six locks to the Caen Hill Marina below, or had decided to call it a night when they'd seen the great flight ascending ahead of them.

Going through a lock wasn't complicated, but a long flight like this could laborious. It took a fit person on the lock gate and a skilled steerer on the boat functioning in reasonable harmony. Open the lower gate from ashore by pushing against a long heavy lever arm. And once the boat had driven in, close the gate and cross to the head of the lock. There, fill the lock by opening the sluice gate above, finally open the upper gate to allow the boat to depart. Repeat fifteen more times.

He followed the upward slope on the paved towpath.

Most of a mile later, he finally knew where he was heading even if he was too tired to think of why.

When he arrived, he faceplanted into his bunk and fell asleep with the sunrise.

133

6

Alice yelped when the face appeared in the window she'd been working on for half the morning. She'd been outlining the window in faux tree-trunk bark.

The face mouthed a *sorry* then disappeared from view. She tugged out a cotton cloth, wiped the paint streak she'd made on the glass, then carefully folded the stain inward before putting it away. The boat swayed slightly as the owner of the face moved about in the cabin and eventually came out on deck. She resettled herself on the small three-legged canvas folding stool on the dock to look at the man standing in the open bow section.

She barely recognized him. It wasn't that she'd given Carl Mason so little thought since he'd given her the job of painting the *Diana*, though she hadn't. It was that he was so transformed.

He'd delivered that boat dressed like any canal boater: jeans, t-shirt, and trainers.

Today he wore very expensive slacks, leather shoes so posh and polished that it was easy to see that they'd had an atypically hard night, and a button-down of unexpected seafoam-green that caused his dark brown eyes to glint like smoked topaz.

She remembered him as handsome.

Now he would look powerful…if he wasn't so wrinkled. The neat wave of dark hair stuck out sideways in a sleep-cowlick. The shirt and slacks had absolutely been slept in.

"What tie do you wear with that gear?" She couldn't help smiling at his rumpled image.

"Uh," he looked down at his chest as if he had no idea what he was wearing, "a colored one?"

She giggled at him. "Try apricot or even a dark coral if you're feeling brave."

Again, that slow self inspection, "I can't say that describes me this morning."

"Go with a sapphire blue then." She turned back to eye the base coat of her faux tree trunk before he could look at her again with that bewildered expression so clear in his dark eyes. "Avoid burgundy unless you want to be mistaken for a Christmas elf."

But even out of the corner of her eye she could see him simply standing there, looking…purposeless. And slightly dazed.

"Oh. I'm sorry. You came to see the progress on your boat." Then she inspected the unpainted length and winced. After that she went out for what Mum called one of her babble-runs. "I'm really sorry that I don't have more to show you. I know it's been weeks, but the old paint job was so awful, and the one under that, and the five or six below them. It's cruel to take wood all the way down like this too often, but it simply needed to be done. I've now laid down a three-layer undercoat that, if treated well, should prevent that being necessary for a long time to come. I did capture a few images of some of the history of the boat as I sanded off layers. They could make an interesting little photo album for your parents. The lowest layer I was able to date was from the 1860s when she was a bawdy-boat."

"A bawdy-boat?"

She could feel her cheeks heat, looking at him fresh from his bed. "*Go for a ride on the canal. Ladies included in the ticket price.* Though maybe they'd rather not know about that piece of its history."

His laugh sounded half normal and half surprised to find itself out wandering along the dock. "No, they'd love it. You want bawdy tales? Read the Greeks, though Chaucer's Wife of Bath would fit in well, too. I can't wait to tell them. You're sure?"

She nodded.

"Isn't that a lark?" He chuckled once more. "But I didn't come to check up on you. It already looks so much better simply being clean."

"Then why did you come in a business suit on a Wednesday morning? You look like the kind of person to be in one of those fancy London high rises."

And his momentary joy collapsed again.

"I...was."

7

———————

And again the confusion returned. Carl wondered if he'd become Alice in Wonderland's hookah-smoking caterpillar, on the edge of transforming, but who the hell knew into what.

He was...here. Talking to the lovely, level-headed painter who was doing something she passionately loved, less than twenty feet from her own floating home that was perhaps the prettiest boat on the whole of the UK canal system.

He too was here, but that was all. His BMW Z4 Roadster was three miles away below the Devizes flight of locks, out of gas on a back country lane. Two hundred kilometers from the nearest change of clothes in his high-rise mid-town condo. And about a kilometer more from the office that filled his life—*had* filled.

No! He'd brought more with him. Of more importance, though he had no idea what. He'd carried a box of the essentials from the car last night and they were here, on the table downstairs. He wondered what the hell he'd found so important from his old life to hand-carry from the car in the

137

middle of the night when he didn't even know where he'd been.

His old life? How could that be his *old* life? His old job, sure. But he wasn't here to change his life.

Alice had returned to her painting. How long had he been standing like a zombified...zombie?

"I'm headed below. I'll try not to rock the boat."

The briefest slide of her hair was the only indication that she'd heard him. She was lost in her world in a way he'd never been lost in his. He was good at it, and he'd liked how that skill made him feel. Earned him a lot of nice pats on the back, then he remembered the bonus and severance package, and a lot of money. But she was absorbed wholly by the art of creating, he glanced down—a tree trunk where there'd never been a tree trunk.

He soft-footed his way below and went to inspect what he'd thought was so precious that he couldn't leave it locked in the car's trunk.

First, Carl scrounged up an old packet of tea from last summer's cruising and a tin of biscuits that Mum always kept handy in case of a breakdown far from a town with a market. Was that it, was he having a breakdown? Because he could think he'd had one, did that mean he was already over it? He checked his watch. Under twelve hours ago. Not really enough to call more than a *lapse*. He'd had a couple of college benders that had lasted longer.

Once his tea was steeping, he dunked a stale biscuit into it and munched as he sat at the table. His family had shared thirty summers of meals here. Mostly good times. Any bouts of sullen teendom had been abandoned ashore at the start of each summer.

Carl opened the small box. It was no bigger than three reams of paper and it was all higgledy-piggledy rather than tightly packed. A little from this drawer or that, rather than gathered by any conscious plan.

A picture of the three of them hamming it up in the cockpit when he was in his teens. He could always start Mum and Dad going with a mangled quote from disparate sources. *Romeo and Juliet* recast with the characters from *Oedipus Rex*. The Old English monster Grendel recast as Juliet's nurse had been one of his favorites. He wished he'd recorded some of the improv plays that they'd spontaneously fabricated together, but they were all lost to happy evenings along the canals. They never happened at home, where the quiet harmony of ancient studies would squeeze down until he'd thought his head about to explode before it would ever break free into the modern world.

Still, below the photo lay his copy of Chaucer's *Canterbury Tales*, in the original Middle English of course, and the eleven surviving plays of Aristophanes *not* in Greek, because he could barely struggle through that. A stack of pads of lined-yellow paper, and a long thin box.

He knew what was inside. He'd always kept it in his top left desk drawer, of college and each job, though he had rarely opened it over the years.

This time he did and looked down at the shining black and gold Waterman pen.

A fine mind needs a fine pen, Mum had said. And Dad had added, *Water Man? You get? Si? Si?* In the voice of Manuel from *Fawlty Towers*. They'd given it to him on their last night together on the narrowboat before he'd left for college.

They understood nothing of what he did in the modern business world as it didn't impinge on their own interests buried not centuries but millennia in the past.

His view of the pen had shifted over the years. At first

fascinated by it, he had attempted to recreate the family farces, though he rarely made it past a page or so. For a while, he'd used it to write witty mash notes on fine parchment with a neat hand that had occasionally earned him laughs—and more often than not had turned into lovely epistemological adventures. Now, if it didn't have a direct plug-in to cloud or display up-to-the-minute business news analyses, it wasn't worth consideration.

Except it was one of the few objects he'd taken with him last night.

Why this out of everything?

8

Once Alice began painting a boat, it was primarily an intuitive process. The forest built quickly. At first only the occasional fox, squirrel, or owl could be glimpsed wandering through.

But then a delicate white horse-like animal, just now wandering out of sight behind a window, showed a shining horn reaching past the far side of the opening.

Two days later, Alice was sure that she spotted a baby griffin preening on a high branch, so she filled it in. The next day, a pair of tiny dragons were roasting marshmallows over each other's flames.

The creatures were often shadowed, barely discernable. But if a person took the time, the forest was populated with everything from dormice to pegasi—though Carl had absently informed her that the proper plural was pegasuses.

With no explanation, he had moved onto the boat.

First, he had departed with a can of gas, then been back a few hours later with a metallic-blue sports car, that he'd called a Misano blue. It wasn't really any proper blue but rather a wandering baby chick lost somewhere in the land not occupied by azure, cobalt, or lapis. Simply because they could make a new color didn't mean they should—it was attention-grabbing, but had no proper emotion attached to it once it had forced her to look its way.

Early the next week, he'd been gone for two days, with hardly a word.

He'd returned with a brand-new two-door Mini Cooper Electric in proper British Racing Green. It was so cute, she wanted to hug it.

It had been stuffed to the gills with boxes, which he was kind enough to leave stacked at the edge of the dock until she was done for the day. When she'd offered a hand loading them aboard, he accepted happily.

"Haven't slept much in a while, so I'll take all the help I can get," as they handed boxes first from dock to boat and then from on deck to down below.

"Why not?" She peeked around the inside of the boat. It was like a slightly rumpled living room, well lived in and comfortable. The interior woodwork had fared far better than the exterior, it looked cherished rather than abandoned.

"Well, let's see." He cracked open a box and began unloading books onto the breakfast nook table. She was bemused by the fact that they were mostly cookbooks. "Seven days ago I had a serious bankroll job, a car that was all about my ego, and a Thames-side apartment meant to make women weep with joy." Then he grimaced. "Uh, sorry about that."

Like she hadn't already known that someone as handsome as Carl had women flocking to him. "Did it work?"

Again the grimace. "Yeah, I guess. At first anyway."

"What happened then?" To keep her hands busy, she

quickly sorted the cookbooks by region, then thought better of it and resorted them by color and began to shelve them close by the kitchen.

"I stopped taking time off from the job. Not a lot happens with women when you never take time off."

"Ah," she didn't comment on her own similar tactics, *keep busy; keep men at bay*. The way men looked at her made their preferences obvious. She'd made enough early mistakes to wait for the quiet and kind ones rather than the handsome men-about-town. Though none had reacted with quite the shocked expression, or the attempt to destroy his narrowboat when he'd first seen her, quite the way Carl had.

"Yep, I bought all the way in. Got a wake-up call the evening before I landed here."

"Seven days ag—"

"Nope!" He cut her off as he dug open the next box and began shifting clothes into a small set of drawers. "Seven anything is too short a timespan for me to be making this kind of change."

"Geological epochs?" she teased him.

"Nope, still way too short," he really smiled at her for the first time since his arrival last week. "How long is one of those anyway?"

She shrugged. Alice actually had no idea either.

"Doesn't matter. So, my life's story of the last seven whatever-really-long-time things?" He broke down the boxes and handed her two bags before waving her toward the kitchen.

She glared at him.

He caught the full blast—and laughed. Her glares were supposed to be more effective than that. "No, sorry."

He was still chuckling and she was considering hitting

him with the smaller bag, which was rather heavy with tin cans.

"I meant for you to stow them on the galley shelves, not cook for me. God, it's been so long since I took the time to cook a meal for myself. I miss it." He nodded toward the cookbooks, cocked his head for a moment at her rainbow-spectrum organization, then nodded again as if that worked for him.

She felt silly for overreacting. "I can barely boil noodles." She'd grown up eating in the pub kitchen each night with Vincent, Edda, and her Mum.

"It always seemed that my parents could live on poetry, as long as it predated the dinosaurs. I learned to cook on this boat as a matter of survival. I'm glad to make us dinner in thanks for your help when we're done here." And he carried another load of belongings down the narrow aisle to the master bedroom.

She began stowing things randomly in the cupboards as his voice drifted to her down the long cabin. What did she know about how to organize a galley? Almost as little as she knew about running a business.

"Seven of those long-time-things ago, I had a job and career that made perfect sense. Six LTTs ago, after driving my car until it entered a fume-free state over in Sells Green, I walked here. For five days, I sat here watching a beautiful woman do something she was completely passionate about. Which left me to wonder what I was passionate about."

"You said you enjoyed your job." They had actually talked very little over those days. Except for sharing quiet sunsets sitting alongside the canal, Carl had rarely left that table in the center cabin except for meals in the pub.

"Right," they met back at the shrinking pile of boxes. "Enjoyed because I was good at it. Not because the job itself was much fun or did anything to inspire me. It made me lots of money and offered only fleeting joy. I bet you aren't like that."

She could only shake her head. "Me? I love thinking of every boat I've ever painted, sailing somewhere along the canals and making their owners happy. It's like I'm spreading cheer over the land. Of course, it doesn't make me wealthy enough to live in a fancy London apartment like yours."

"Would you want to if it did?"

"You're joking, right?" He didn't look like he was though. "Uh, no. I like the size of my life." And she was once again reminded *that* was going to change in two more weeks, one way or another. Vincent insisted they were going. Edda had tried talking to her as well, but something inside Alice knotted past tolerance each time the subject came up until she could neither speak nor hear.

The unchanging arc of her life since birth was about to be broken. Whether or not she took over the business, her life would never be the same.

"Yeah, it doesn't fit me anymore either. That's why I traded in the car and sold the apartment. That's where I was over the last two days. This is now the size of my life." He patted the stack of boxes and looked around the boat. "The only thing I don't have is clear knowledge whether I'm being brilliantly insightful or having a mental breakdown."

9

─────────

Alice too wondered that, about herself, as she discovered a red squirrel family perched in an ash tree on the aft quarter of the *Diana.*

Unlike his first days on the boat, when he'd rarely spoken, Carl had become relaxed and voluble. The two faces of drama: tragedy and comedy. He'd received one but decided to consciously make it into the other.

When she'd asked over dinner what he was planning to do, he had shrugged. *No need to rush, between the job and condo sale I'm set for quite a while. Years. Maybe,* and he'd laughed in surprise, *decades if this becomes the scale of my lifestyle.*

And while he'd spoken, he'd toyed with a small metal case that rested on the edge of the table.

10

————

They spent another week practically cohabitating on the boat. *Practically* because he slept inside at night and she worked on the outside during the day. He was often gone from breakfast to dinner, always afoot with a small pack. The little green Mini never moved from its parking spot. Snooping through the boat's window, she saw that the small box was never there on the table during the day.

In the mornings they'd share coffee, a pastry, maybe a few words as the day started quietly. She appreciated that, as she was typically organizing her night's thinking into what would become the day's painting.

Dinner, however, was a different affair. He made sumptuous meals or organized a gourmet picnic that they would take to the head of the Devizes Flight of locks to watch the narrowboats make the traverse. He'd been trained by two classicists and she'd learned history through art. For hours they would sit and discuss topics that ranged across Europe from the Socrates to Banksy. Half the time it was reality and half more fanciful than even the creatures on the *Diana* or the *Alice*.

The first time she'd kissed him had been along the Devizes Flight up the Caen Hill. He'd been creating a fairy tale made of King Arthur's knights calling up the ghost of Socrates to help them determine a battle plan, but the old man kept insisting that it was time to discuss shadows created by the flickering fire.

When Carl had revealed that Socrates had actually been taking whispered instruction from a dormouse napping on his shoulder, she'd been unable to help herself. She'd kissed him.

The first time she'd slept with him, it had been in her bed aboard the *Alice,* which he'd been surprised to find had been painted very simply as a cozy burrow that a badger or hedgehog or even a Hobbit—if it wouldn't be in the wrong story—might enjoy.

It wasn't that he was the best lover she'd ever had, though he was. Rather, Carl's bravery at forging a new path, whatever it might be, had lit something inside her that she didn't recognize. But she rather liked it.

"I've never been a deep thinker," she informed him one night when she woke to find the moonlight dancing through her bedroom windows.

"Nor I in my past."

"But you are now?"

Carl considered a while with his head upon her breast. "I'm not sure. I have a theory."

"Filled with fabulous creatures and peculiar non sequiturs?"

His light laugh rippled from his jaw to her breastbone. "I don't think so but I can try if you'd like."

"I *love* your stories." And she did. Whether he was telling tales of fancy, of history, or of some event in his life, his voice, his *words* carried her there. To that place that built so richly in her imagination.

"Uh, thanks," he said it a little stiffly, but before she could ask why he hurried on. "There's only one kind of stupid, but lately I've been thinking that there are many kinds of smart."

"I barely made it through secondary, except for my art classes." She wanted to be more than merely pretty. She could feel his London Business School masters even if he never hinted at the vast chasm that it created between them.

"That's irrelevant. You are utterly brilliant."

All she could do was scoff at him. "You just like being in my bed."

"I do, but that's not my point. Seriously, Alice," she could feel Carl's smile in the night. "And how many times did Alice tell herself to be serious in Wonderland of all places. Anway, you have this amazing painting ability."

"That's a skill, not an intelligence."

"No argument, but you didn't let me finish. You apply that skill with an emotional intelligence and a sensitivity that makes you loved up and down the length of the canal. I ran into your bald-headed captain of *Samson's Strength* one day when I was walking along the canal. And despite a complete lack of understanding of Biblical mythos, he couldn't offer enough praise when I mentioned you were doing my parents' boat. Yet it looks nothing like mine, which looks nothing like yours. In fact, I've been trying to spot your work as I walk past the boats and the only common factor I've found is that they utterly stand out. Each person I ask, confirms that it is your work and how much they love it. I have no idea how you do that, but it's utterly brilliant."

She kept her thoughts to herself on those points. Unlike most men, Carl never made her feel stupid or uneducated or ignorant. But brilliant? Not by any measure she understood. Time for a subject change.

"What color is your intelligence then?"

"I thought it was business. I understand the shape and nature of how businesses fit together. But the more I think about all those years, the more I think that falls into the skills category."

And that's when she heard the fear in his voice. He wasn't blithely dumping one lifestyle and tumbling into another. He was seeking more, more of himself. That was the moment Alice knew she had embarked on no simple fling. Her lover was afraid, which only made him all the more brave. She didn't know what his *intelligence* was—beyond convincing her that she was wonderful in more ways than she'd ever imagined—but she knew he possessed more of it than any man she'd ever been with.

She slid her arms around him and held him close. Held him until he fell asleep, leaving neither of them convinced.

But as she stroked his hair and watched the moonlight shifting through the tall trees bordering the canal, perhaps they were both hopeful.

11

"Alice," Vincent's voice landed somewhere between pleading and annoyance and he interrupted her work on the outer side of the bow.

She tried to find last night's hope, but despite whatever intelligence that Carl was so convinced she possessed, she wasn't very good at finding it.

"One week. Edda is ready, the boat is ready. When we hand over the pub, we hand over our flat above as well. The business is yours whether you want it or not. If you decide to close it, that will be up to you."

She neither wanted it nor knew what she would do without it. She certainly didn't want to be the one responsible for shuttering Vincent's life's work.

"I put no boats on the schedule, but there's already a waiting list as long as the summer. You could keep three of you busy if you wanted to hire some assistants."

That meant employees, which meant payrolls and taxes and more supplies and—

Alice bit down hard on the panic.

She'd be done with the *Diana* by the end of this week as

well. What then? Would Carl float away and be gone? Who would fill the empty mooring that Vincent and Edda left behind?

"I'm sorry, Vincent. I shouldn't have delayed you. But I don't know what I'm doing and—" her voice was climbing toward hysteria, so she bit it off hard.

Against his normal practice of disappearing during the day, Carl had come back. He was standing at the head of the dock looking quizzically at the two of them standing by the *Diana's* bow.

"Um, should I come back later?"

Alice could only look down at her knees and shake her head miserably. Vincent had given her two months' warning and for all her vaunted *intelligence,* she'd taken no action.

"Is everything okay?"

She shook her head again.

12

———

And that, Carl knew, was his cue. Though he had no idea of his first line now that he'd made his grand entrance. That would teach him to forget his slicker when it was raining out.

He sat on the gunnel of the *Diana* and faced Alice perched on her little painter's stool. Vincent, who he'd shared a beer with as they'd both watched Alice work late yesterday evening, stood—at a loss—a few steps away. By some silent pact, he hadn't asked a single question about Alice or how she was related to the old man. Instead, Vincent had used a style not so different from one of Mum's gentle inquisitions. It had Carl spilling much of his past, though none of his current doubts.

"You two at odds feels very wrong. Can I help?"

Alice's head remained down and Vincent scowled at him. Well, this was a good start—if he wanted Dante's Virgil to lead him on a ramble through hell.

"I've known her since three months after she was conceived, what would you know that could possibly help?"

Vincent snapped. Skip the ramble, Carl was being dragged straight into the ninth circle.

"I know nothing about what's going on so maybe I can lend an impartial ear." Only the rain pattering on the shed roof's skylights answered him.

Vincent grunted then dropped back to sit on the fresh-painted boat in the other slip.

"No!" But his call was too late and Vincent's butt hit wet paint.

He shoved to his feet leaving an additional palm print on the fresh paint to match the stripe on his bum.

"That'll teach this old man. Beginner's mistake." He fished a cotton cleanup rag from Alice's stack and used a splash of turps to clean his hand.

"I'll fix it," Alice mumbled miserably. "It's all my fault that—"

"Hell you will, Alice. I painted this boat. I sat my old bum down on it, so I'll fix it. But not until we fix this." He flapped a sheaf of papers at her that he'd tucked under his arm while cleaning his hand.

"May I?" Carl held out a hand.

Vincent glared at him before practically slapping them in Carl's face as he handed them over. "Okay, Mr. Businessman, you go ahead and find a single goddamn thing wrong with those." Then he stalked away down the dock muttering to himself about having to remix the paint colors.

Carl had analyzed five-hundred-page contracts covering massive mergers and acquisitions. This was a half page transference to Alice of all rights belonging to K&A Lion, Boat Painters. Its property, assets, client list, bank accounts, and appointment book. For—

"Ten pounds?"

Alice still hadn't spoken.

"And you aren't leaping at this because...?" In a past life, he'd have finished that with *you're stupid.*

"Because I'm stupid," she finished it for him. "Go ahead and say it, I heard the thought."

"I didn't say it because you aren't."

"But that's what you're thinking, right?"

He flashed back to last night's discussion in her arms about not being a deep thinker. He hadn't been. His education, business acumen, women, his *life* had always come to him easily, so why waste time thinking about it. These last weeks he'd done more deep thinking than the whole of his life combined.

"No-oo. Not the new me, anyway. The old me might have, but the more time I think about him, the more I'm convinced he was an idiot and I'm better shut of him."

For the first time, she raised her gaze enough to glance briefly at him with those piercing blue eyes. "There's only one me. This one," she waved at the *Diana*, which wasn't going to be just the envy of the canal, it was going to be the envy of an art museum. "Not that one," she waved at the papers in his hand.

He looked at the other pages. Legal deed to the property. Most recent balance statement that showed a nicely profitable business of long standing. And a multi-page long waiting list of boat name, brief job description, and contact information. The final page was a schedule sheet for the two slips...and it was blank. Vincent had scheduled nothing ahead, awaiting Alice's decision.

"Is there some catch here I don't understand? Does Vincent have some hold over you or—"

"He's the best man who ever lived!" And there was a fire in her eyes that was completely new to him.

"Should I be jealous?" Carl did his best to make it a joke. "Not sure I like the idea of someone other than me holding that much of your heart."

It seemed to work. Alice reached out a hand and brushed his cheek. "Mum landed here as a pregnant nineteen-year-old. Vincent and Edda took us in. Raised me like I was one of his own. His son died in Afghanistan by the time I was ten. Vincent gave me..." she shrugged "...everything."

"And now he's trying to give you the business."

"Yes."

"And?"

"The *business*. I'm a business idiot. All I've ever done or known to do was paint boats. Do you think it makes one instant of sense that I've spent six weeks exclusively on your boat? Budget?" She splayed her fingertips off her temple hard enough to foof a brief wave through her hair. "I blew that four weeks ago and didn't care."

"I'll pay the difference."

She shrugged. "I'm not asking for—"

"I'll pay the difference. I already guessed that and told Vincent. It's worth it to have the boat done right for my parents."

"Oh. But that's not the point. Vincent is leaving. He always ran the business."

Carl stared down at the papers. He could run this operation on twenty minutes a day. Schedule, money, budget, and stay out of the painters' way. Add a couple staff and it could be seriously profitable.

But it wasn't his place.

If this relationship ended, he'd be gone and she'd be stuck with a disaster of his making. He couldn't do that to her. Nor did he like the sound of the *ending* part of that thought.

He had never so enjoyed being with a woman. Every moment he was with her, new vistas of possibility opened up for him. Would he have walked away from London if he hadn't had the vision of Alice living along the K&A Canal that was so filled with happy memories of his own? Probably not. He'd certainly received enough calls from headhunters to join any number of prestigious firms. In the last week, New York, Tokyo, and Singapore had all called.

These few precious weeks had been an awakening in every clichéd sense of the word. He'd spent long mornings walking along the canal and long afternoons writing ideas with that pen Mum had given him. He'd have to switch over to a computer soon, but the framework for a novel—a fun, fantasy romp filled with goddesses and humans—had somehow passed through the filter of falling down the *Alice's* Lewis Carroll-type rabbit hole was all there. He was rediscovering his youthful joy of writing something other than business proposals.

That too was easy to lay at Alice's feet.

"You inspire me," the words slipped out in a whisper to dance upon the morning light.

"I what?"

He focused more clearly upon her. "You. You're the one I want to tell my stories to. You're the one who keeps opening doors I didn't know existed. These last weeks I've been… happy! Happy without knowing I was sad before. Except I wasn't sad. So I suppose you've made me happ*ier*. Please tell me how to make you happier."

13

____

Happier? Had she ever been *un*happier?

Alice had never in her life argued with Vincent before. He was father, mentor, and confidante-best friend all rolled into one. When her snarky teen hormones had her and Mum in a stand-off, Vincent was the one she'd turned to.

"I'm hurting him. I know I'm hurting him. And it's killing me." She couldn't keep the anguish out of her voice. She'd never been able to. Her emotions always shot straight to the surface before she even knew they were there.

Carl took her hand, then brushed at the tears she hadn't known were there.

He waited, but she couldn't think of any words to say, even if she could speak. All she could do was hold onto his hand and wonder if he could keep her from drowning in her own inadequacy. Wouldn't Lewis Carroll have the last laugh if she did—a real lake of tears.

"Okay, I could make a stupid offer, but I'm not going to. I could step in as a business partner and run it for you, but we're at the beginning of us. I really like this beginning, but I know that's all it is. It's good enough that I can't wait for the next step, but we aren't there. So that isn't the answer."

She really liked their beginning too. No one had ever made her feel so appreciated for herself. But he was right, it wasn't the answer. And that made her feel that much closer to Carl that he saw that—rather than trying to *rescue the poor little bird*. Still, it wasn't enough.

Carl flipped through the sheaf of papers then laughed a little to himself. "Let's try twenty questions."

She had a thousand. What she didn't have was any answers.

"First, is there anything in the world you'd rather be doing than painting boats? Fine art? Dance? Modeling, which you certainly have the looks for? Nuclear scientist?"

The last elicited a laugh that was only partly choking sob. "Anything in the world? How would I know? I've never been anywhere except along the canals. Mum and I joined Vincent and Edda on holidays, but they were always boating holidays."

"Nowhere exotic? Not even down the rabbit hole?"

She smiled toward her own boat. "Not outside my thoughts. You?"

"A lot of places...for work. Mostly I saw loads of near-identical conference rooms. Not much of anywhere else for me either."

Alice began studying Carl's fingers because she could feel him studying her face and doing some of that deep thinking of his. They were good hands. Not callused, but strong. She liked the way they felt in hers. She liked the way she felt in his arms. And she'd miss him when—

She gasped. She never thought ahead about anything.

"What?"

"When I finish your boat, where do you go? Does all this

end?" It felt as if her heart had been painted over with a hard acrylic.

"My parents' moorage is about half a mile away."

"And you're staying on the boat?"

"Until I think of something better. They're aboard three months a year, but I have my own room even then."

Again she found a watery laugh, just a little louder than the passing of a narrowboat out on the canal. "See? I don't think ahead. I never thought about you leaving when I finished your boat. Does that sound like a businesswoman?"

"Business isn't your *intelligence.* I could set up some simple steps for you to manage it. Vincent's been doing it so long, I doubt if it's even conscious for him, but I could teach you."

"But if it doesn't work then..." she sighed, "Then I'm right back where I started."

14

And Carl burst out laughing.

Alice could not imagine how what she'd said was in any way funny.

"Sorry, okay. I think I have an answer. Care to take a trip down the rabbit hole with me?"

"I...suppose."

"Good. Do you have ten pounds on you?"

She fished a note out of her pocket and handed it over.

"Sign there," he handed her Vincent's papers. Then he reached into his pocket and pulled out the small metal case. Inside was a lovely fountain pen. An artist's, no, a *writer's* fountain pen. It had his name scribed on it and M&D. "Mum and Dad," he explained.

She was halfway to signing it when she caught herself, "No! Wait!"

He placed his hand lightly on the back of hers and guided it toward the signature line. "Trust me."

And for some reason, she signed.

He took everything back and shook her hand. "Congratulations."

"What have you done to me? This doesn't feel like a rabbit hole, it feels like a bottomless pit."

"All the best rabbit holes do," he smiled. "You now legally own K&A Lion, Boat Painters."

"But—" He stopped her with a finger upon her lips.

"Now comes the rabbit hole part. Ready? Let's go traveling."

"What?" He wasn't making any sense.

Carl smiled. "Let's jump in together. Narrowboat through Scotland, ride motorcycles across the Australian Outback, go to a small Italian cliff town to hike the hills and eat a different flavor of gelato every day for a month. Let's do something, together. Let's find out if we can sail along the same channel."

She liked the sound of that. A lot. She had spent very little money on herself and Vincent had always paid her a good wage.

"And then, whenever you want, you can come back here. Sell the business and start something new. Hire a partner who *does* know the business side. Turn it into your own private studio. Whatever you want. There's good equity here. That means you now have some money and the property is all paid for. Vincent will have done what he wants to most, he'll have set you up as well as he could before retiring. What you do from there is up to you."

Alice didn't know where to look. But she could see many surprising things she'd never noticed before. Over the last five years Vincent had re-roofed the boat shed, had all of the rotten timbers in the docks replaced, even upgraded what little office equipment and paint storage they needed. He'd done his best to fix it up...for her.

And she *did* love it here. If her life could be spent

painting the unending variety of narrowboats, it would be a life she enjoyed.

She also saw a flash of a boy and girl racing along these same docks she had as a child, a place where she'd found so much happiness and contentment.

The man. The one who even now sat waiting for her. It was easy to see him here too. Writing his tales. Novels, plays, magazine stories. It wouldn't matter, because she knew that Carl would find the joy in anything he did.

She watched him as he stood and moved to meet Vincent halfway along the dock. He handed over the papers, the ten-pound note, and shook Vincent's hand. Vincent looked as if he was going to cry with happiness.

Yes, she *would* jump down the rabbit hole with Carl. They would...go see the art of Paris and Florence.

But then she would come home.

Here.

And paint her joy.

But first, there was a Phoenix peeking over Diana's shoulder, near to bursting with the desire to come to life.

CARVED FROM SAND

ABOUT THIS STORY

Local Gloucester artist Morgan Henry built a career carving sand. Upon the arrival of a magnificent racing yacht off the beach, he alters his latest contest entry to match. Little does he know that his past skippers the boat.

Mary Elizabeth sailed away from Gloucester and made her name on the ocean racing circuit. She never once looked back. Yet for reasons beyond her understanding, she returns.

On the beach, in a sand sculpture conceived by a boy but carved by a man, she discovers that her past and her future are more connected than she could possibly imagine.

1

———————

Morgan flicked the kill switch and the pounding stopped. His arms were buzzing from manhandling the gas-powered jumping jack tamper for much of the morning. Thank God he was done with that phase of the build. The early phases of building a competition-level sand castle required much more than a plastic shovel—a stage he'd never truly enjoyed. He had his sand prepped. Now the fun began.

Shoving back the earmuffs, he was assaulted by the clatter and engine roar of others near him. Three of the other fifteen competitors were still compacting their sand. The rest were shoveling more sand into their next layer of frames prior to more compaction.

Only Romero had already shed the topmost layer of forms and begun shaping. Nobody sculpted sand as fast as Romero. It was a pity he didn't like Romero's work. He had a whole Mexican Day of the Dead macabre vibe. He also colored his sand with clays and food coloring, which was technically acceptable, but felt wrong to Morgan.

He was a traditionalist down to the soles of his callused

feet and believed that the coloring hid the actual artistry of the carving itself.

Fifteen feet up in the air atop his sculpture offered an exceptional view. This was his home sand, Good Harbor Beach, Gloucester, Mass. He'd grown up less than two miles away and had spent much of his youth riding his bike here. Half a mile of smooth beach sand, hard-packed by the tides, backed by dunes and with the whole sweep of the Atlantic straight ahead. Interrupted only by tiny Salt Island to the north, which connected to the shore by a rocky sandbar at dead low tides.

They had four days to build their sculptures, and it was already the morning of the second day. But the weather was perfect, a light overcast and only a vague breeze. The sand wouldn't dry too fast.

He knelt down and poked his fingers into the topmost compacted layer. Almost no give at all—just perfect.

The organizers had done a good job, trucking in rougher glacial sand for better holding ability. Beach sand was typically too smooth, all of its sharp, holding edges worn off by the pounding of the sea. Exceptional sand, one percent water, and hard compaction. He liked the feeling of this one.

He glanced down the line. Sure enough, the pinnacle of Romero's sculpture was taking on the shape of a battered top hat. So predictable. Morgan's theory was to stay fresh by constantly changing and growing his artistic style.

The long beach was busy for a weekday. Of course, it always was in the summer. He spotted a cluster of bicycles up by the wooden walking bridge from Eastern Point that arced over the salt marsh drainage channel. How many times as a kid had he parked his own bike there?

Mom had always told him to get a life. Dad had been a professional surfer in his youth and understood Morgan's need to be at the beach. But with them gone, Morgan knew he was straining the limits of what his career could be. It had taken a decade to build up to going pro. Sponsors now paid his way to competitions all over the East Coast—the visiting master sculptor. More money on the side for teaching classes. He'd even done a couple of West Coast competitions on his own dime but almost always ended up in the money. First prize could net him ten grand for a week's work. Too bad there weren't competitions like this one every week. Of course that way lay travel burnout and severe sand rash.

He was at some tipping point. Balanced as lightly as one dry sand grain atop another. Morgan had no idea what lay to either side. After this week, nothing remained to tie him to Gloucester except memories.

Focus on the here and now.

This beach was a good one without being a zoo like Coney Island or Hampton Beach up in New Hampshire. The latter was thoroughly epitomized by a hundred kitsch shops packed tighter than wet sand, including seventeen t-shirt shops in the main mile (he'd lost count after that and hadn't bothered to check out the back streets), at least as many overpriced restaurants, and even a deep-fried Oreo stand of all madness. Not his kind of scene.

Here at Good Harbor there was the hot dog and ice cream concessions stand, and nothing else. Rolling grass dunes, tidal marsh, and an incredible stretch of beauty. It was a foolish investment for the parks department, any income draw from the spectacle of the competition should be shared over a range of merchants. But this beach was well isolated from the rest of the retail in the area. Not his bother.

As he looked out to sea, a big sloop eased up toward the

beach. Its lone mast seemed to etch the sky. The dark red hull and long lines made it look incredibly fast even as it came up into the wind and dropped an anchor. The rattle of the chain dropping overboard reached the beach during a chance pause of the various power tampers around him. He noticed that his wasn't the only pair of eyes that appreciated the boat. Growing up around Gloucester Harbor, he knew a purebred ocean racer when he saw one.

He looked down at the sand below his feet.

Morgan had initially planned to do Venus on the half-shell. Part Botticelli's *The Birth of Venus* and part the Philip José Farmer spoof novel of Kurt Vonnegut's character Kilgore Trout.

Now?

Again he eyed the lovely boat offshore.

There wasn't time to break down the forms and restack the sand.

But...

If he heeled the boat over to shift the mast to the side, he could carve that beauty out of what he already had.

Almost.

One more bucket. He'd need one perfect bucket of sand atop his current structure for the masthead. He glanced over at Romero working feverishly on his hat brim. One bucket would also make his own sculpture taller than Romero's by several inches, making it the tallest on the beach. Yes, he was good with that.

There was a lot of excess sand in the lower layers that he'd built with a different design in mind, but he'd think about that when he'd carved down far enough.

One more good look at the boat, just in case it left before he was done. Once it was firmly fixed in his mind, he clambered down the tiers hauling the jumping jack tamper with him. Mixing the perfect bucket of sand was second nature. Hauling the sixty-five-pound bucket fifteen feet in the air was as well.

A glance at the boat, he doublechecked the bucket's position for the new design in his mind's eye, and flipped it into place. As he worked to ease it free, he saw in his memory that a single figure had been diving off the side of the big ocean racer.

2

––––––––

Mary came ashore on the warm haven of sand and wanted to simply lie there hugging it.

At the end of her trans-Atlantic race, she'd never actually gone ashore in New York. She'd meant to. After placing second in the solo race from Calais, France to the Brooklyn Bridge, she'd definitely planned to. There would have been good parties after the crossing. And she hadn't placed second in any *mere* women's division; she'd placed second overall to Thierry Montagne who was a masterful skipper. Masterful enough to beat her by thirty-seven minutes after the long crossing.

He had stepped over onto her boat on arrival, offered her a hug, and held her hand up to the cheering crowd that had packed the Brooklyn waterfront park. It had been kind, and he was always kind, except between the starting gun and the finish line when he was a ferocious and highly skilled competitor.

But then potential sponsors had come aboard. And newscasters. And boat geeks who began poking through everything that was hers. And women telling her that she was the perfect symbol of the modern powerful woman. And—

She'd shooed them all away, let slip the lines, and sailed toward home before the third-place finisher had passed the Verrazzano-Narrows Bridge. It was stupid, she knew. The sponsors alone were a key means to continuing to do the one thing she understood and loved.

But she wasn't anybody's symbol of anything. She was...herself.

Once here, not possessing enough patience to unship the dinghy, she had dived over the side and swum ashore.

In the shallow water, she now sat as she often had as a child, chest deep in the water, the low waves only occasionally splashing against her chin. There was something different about the water here. It simply felt right.

Straight ahead lay nothing until the Azores and the bulge of Africa. At her back lay her home town. She hadn't been back to Gloucester in a long time.

Mary tried to imagine why she was back at all. Her parents were gone. Her friends were other sailors, not the now total strangers from Gloucester. Even Vincenzo her first sailing instructor had died of old age, slipping beneath the waves of sleep and never reemerging, to give him his sailorly metaphor. His daughter had sent Mary the scrap album he'd kept of all of her races. *All* of them, even ones she hadn't recalled right back to her days ruling the Mass Bay Sailing Junior Championships.

She'd visited him only the month before he'd died, but hadn't been back in the decade since.

So why now?

For an overpriced hot dog and a pre-packaged ice cream cone?

Could be.

She climbed to her feet and did her best to squeeze the water out of her hair. Really facing the land for the first time, it was as if nothing had changed. The wide beach, low salt-grass dunes behind. She knew that beyond that was the most expensive parking lot for a long way around. But the city pumped some of that money back into the beach; the sand was perfectly groomed except for a thin line of seaweed at the high tide line.

And inland...

She cocked her head and heard her neck joints crack.

Great wooden structures were lined up along the beach. Some over a story high, all roughly pyramidal in form. She saw someone had carved what looked like a black, actually black, battered top hat; his body blocking what he was working on below that.

Some were still shoveling sand, a few were breaking open the upper layers of their structures. She hit the concession stand, where the hot dogs looked so All-American that she ordered two, which would give her indigestion later but she didn't care. With one slathered in mustard and relish, and the other in ketchup—because only the grossly crass mixed all three—she went back to sit on the dune edge and watch the sand sculptors.

These were serious folks. Nobody was scooping together a bucket of wet sand and scraping a hole in it, about her level of sandcastle mastery.

Up close, she could see that Mr. Top Hat was shaping a grinning gray-white skull. At least she hoped it would be grinning when he reached that far.

A woman down the row cursed when she accidentally batted her prepared sand tower with the framing board she'd just removed, and created a small cascade of sand off the exposed face. After careful inspection of a drawing, she wiped her brow and proceeded to remove the other three sides. *Damage fixable.*

Near to where she'd landed, a long, rangy man with dirty blond hair to his shoulders trapped by a red bandana worked on the tallest of the piles. He had a beard just thick enough to not be a scruffy Captain Jack Sparrow pirate. Standing high in the air, he kept looking out to sea.

Looking toward her boat, the *Niles P.* She'd named it for the pond on the East Gloucester peninsula where she'd swum so often as a kid.

He wore no shirt, showing off his good muscles. Then he reached into his toolbelt—Captain Jack with a toolbelt was a nice combo—pulled out a palette knife and began carving. With quick confidant strokes he began cutting away at the cylinder of sand that topped his structure. It didn't take a genius to see her mast top emerging from the sand.

Except with far more detail than would be visible from this far away. The head block pulleys appeared rapidly from the sand. With a different tool, a wooden school ruler wielded like a saw, he made tiny marks along the exposed edges that would be the wire stays. That was a crazy level of detail, especially considering the huge amounts of sand trapped inside the lower plywood tiers.

He was almost frantic as he broke off the first layer of forms and tossed them down, nearly landing them on her toes.

"Sorry," he mumbled, but kept working without really turning.

It seemed that he was shedding an immense amount of sand. Mr. Top Hot and Creepy Skull was carving away small layers, but Captain Jack was shedding whole slabs, like the calving glaciers she'd seen in Greenland. Mr. THCS had been well ahead of the Captain when she'd arrived. But every time he paused to check his art against his drawing with level and tape measure, the man copying her sailboat in sand never hesitated. He was soon farther along despite all of the extra carving.

Perhaps he'd changed his mind when he saw her boat. Her boat certainly hadn't been there when he'd been piling the sand up.

Partway down the sail, just even with the spreaders, he froze. "Dammit! What was the number?" He glared offshore at her boat as if he could read the number on the furled sail.

"Thirty-four," she called up to him.

"Thirty-four what?" he turned around looking for the voice that had spoken to him, except he was scanning the sky around him at his level, not looking down at the people below. She was not the only one come to watch the carving, even at this early stage.

"Thirty-four is the number on my sail."

"Your sail?" He finally looked down at her. "Madonna Mother of God." His jaw went slack. And that's how she knew the boy now grown into the pirate.

"You haven't called me that since grade school, Mr. Morgan Henry the Backward Pirate." Which had been her nickname for him. He'd taken great pride in almost being Sir Henry Morgan, the real pirate's namesake. It fit; he'd grown up to look rather piratical. Calling him the backward pirate had helped keep him in his place as a boy. Not really —unlike her, he'd been irrepressible—but she'd liked to think of it that way back then.

"Mary Elizabeth Thomas," he breathed it like a prayer. He'd always liked that her first and middle name had matched Sir Henry Morgan's wife.

It had led to a great excuse to tease each other

mercilessly as they were growing up. Of course, Sir Henry had married his first cousin, also a Morgan, but what did they know about genetics back then.

"Wait!" He swung an arm to point out to sea and almost knocked the top off the sail he'd been carving. "Your boat?"

She nodded, and bit into her hot dog. Mary wasn't quite sure where the first one had gone, but this second one tasted damn good. Summers spent here as a little girl flooded back. She'd never belonged, but being with others even though she rarely spoke had been better than the achingly empty Niles Beach backed by the eight or ten mansions that owned its length.

He looked like a string puppet. First staring down at her, then twisting to look out at her boat, then back to her, and finally down at the vast pile of sand he stood on.

The backward pirate wasn't the gawky kid she remembered. He'd been bullied plenty in school for his light build and sharp mind. She'd been a jock, already winning sailboat races by the time she was eight. A misfit, but winning for the school had been her protective shield. He'd had nothing except his artistic flair, which had always attracted the worst attention. Their mutual teasing was the closest either of them probably had to a friendship growing up.

Until her parents had shipped her off to Milton Academy starting in seventh grade. They hadn't wanted a kid underfoot and Milton had the best sailing program of any prep school up to her parents' hoity-toity standards. Losing her one semi-ally, her only protection at Milton had been to be the best. She'd never been a straight-A student, but nobody beat her on the water—ever.

She hadn't thought of the backward pirate much since, having done her best to block Gloucester out of her mind.

This time when he stared at her once more, she saw no sign of the gawky kid. He was studying her, not as a surprising piece of his past fetched up like a battered bit of driftwood but as if he was trying to memorize her.

"Could you drop your right shoulder a bit?"

She raised it as if she was the *Hunchback of Notre Dame* and he laughed.

"You always were a contrarian. Just drop it, please."

"Well, because you said please," she dropped it all the way until she was slouching against the sand like a melted Dali clock.

He laughed then called down, "Hold that for a sec."

Mary was tempted to move simply to annoy him, but he was no longer looking at her. Instead he was intently studying the sand below his feet.

At a loud curse from two sculptures down, Mary jolted upright.

Morgan didn't react at all except to mutter softly, "Saw that coming."

The woman who had smacked the top layer of her sand tower with the board was staring at the cascading collapse of the exposed layer as whole sections of sand sloughed off and spilled over the lower tiers to land on the beach below.

3

———

Morgan's attempts to reconcile the grown-up Mary Elizabeth, the sailboat, and the yet unworked sand tower beneath his feet wasn't happening.

He couldn't begin to count the times he'd thought of her. She'd been his one friend, a fact he hadn't known until she was gone. His only touchstone of sanity beyond the front door of his family home. He in a crappy house out with the other broke artists of Rocky Neck had always had support and laughter, if not much money. She in her majestic Niles Pond Victorian where nothing was happy. What a difference a mile made.

She hadn't even come back for the double funeral of her parents. Some company had cleared out the house with no sign of her. One day up for sale and gone the next.

Her hair was still sunlight blonde and her eyes crystalline blue but Mary had grown into her angular face. The girl, always so serious and intent, now had elegant features. As the wet t-shirt and sleek one-piece underneath showed, she still retained the power that had always radiated from her once she'd discovered sailing and become a workout queen.

That the gorgeous racing boat anchored offshore, with no sign of anyone else aboard, was hers somehow made sense. Racing across oceans fit Mary Elizabeth right down to the, uh, ocean's floor. Maybe. Not really.

No, the only thing that truly made sense in his head at the moment was the sand. He'd always understood the sand.

And now, with perhaps more clarity than he'd ever had in his life, he could see exactly what waited to be exposed in the layers below.

"Please don't go anywhere," he whispered, then selected a small, triangular cake icing palette knife to etch the number thirty-four into the sail before moving to break away the next lower set of frames. Again he almost dropped them on her where she sat below.

4

—————

At some point, she handed him a chocolate ice cream cone.

"Nutty Buddy. I always loved these." He peeled back the paper and bit into the hard chocolate-and-nut topping.

"I remember."

That brought him the rest of the way back from wherever he'd gone. The really good sandcastles sucked him in, until he lost all track of time and place. Until there was only himself and sand.

Taking a spray bottle in his free hand, he circled the sculpture looking for dry spots. He'd broken his way down through four tiers of plywood forms—eight vertical feet done, past halfway. He had the jib and main sail formed as if they were drawing full wind. A spritz here, a spritz there. That should be enough to keep it stable through the night.

The night?

He twisted to look to the west. The sun was gone beyond the dunes and the hill past that. The thin overcast had stuck, and the far horizon glowed in an arc of red.

"Wow!" he rolled his shoulders, which ached but in a job-well-done sort of way, then clambered down the last two layers to look up at what he'd achieved so far. The sails were close to the theoretical limit for sand. He'd made the base of each thick, he'd had to, but from either side he'd held the illusion of the curve drawing to the wind.

Spreaders could only be a suggestion, several feet of sand sticking straight to the side simply wasn't possible without illegal artificial supports.

Tomorrow. Tomorrow, he'd start to carve the body of the boat and...

"I'm heading home."

It took him a moment to shake loose the image of the grand Victorian on Niles Pond. "Oh, to your boat."

"Yes. Maybe I'll see you tomorrow."

"I'll be right here."

She nodded, and with a wave was striding off into the low surf to swim back out to her boat.

Yeah, he licked where the Nutty Buddy was melting over the backs of his fingers making them all sticky.

Yeah. Reconciling the return of Mary Elizabeth Thomas was something that was going to take a lot more work than any sand sculpture.

5

———

She should simply sail away. If she had half a brain, she would. Why the hell had she come back here anyway? To stir up all of those oh-so-happy memories she'd spent a lifetime blocking out?

Pacing the length of her boat, she began her routine nightly check when not under way. The main and jib were properly stowed. The bungee cord was on the genny halyard so that it wouldn't slap against the aluminum mast in the night. Her three-sixty-degree at-anchor light was shining bright white. She set the depth gauge to wake her if the anchor slipped and she drifted into shallow waters. Weather radar, forecasts, and barometer all predicted a quiet few days.

Everything was shipshape.

Except her.

Sixty feet she paced up one side of the deck and down the other but couldn't come to rest. When she finally forced herself to lie down in the cockpit, she watched the sky, a star here, another there through gaps in the overcast. Though she knew the night sky well, there was rarely a large enough clear area at once for her to identify them. Yet she watched for hours until the cool evening finally drove her below deck to her bunk.

The seagulls, who were stupid enough to think she might have been a fishing boat and greeted her arrival so loudly, had long since flown off to sleep elsewhere.

She'd been done with Gloucester long before her parents had shipped her to Milton. A mere hour from home, and not once had they come to see her race. They were too lost in their own misery. By the time of her graduation, she doubted they were capable of making the journey at all. She'd only gone home once, that first Christmas. It was not a mistake she'd ever repeated.

Alcohol Poisoning, and Gunshot Wound read the official death certificates when they'd reached her during her first stint as navigator in the Sydney Hobart Race. Mom drank herself to death and Dad must have realized that he couldn't survive with no one left to fight with. He'd been sober enough to shoot himself, but not sober enough to do it well. It must have been an ugly way to die, slow and alone with Mom's corpse beside him.

The family money had been deep enough, the property valuable enough, the estate antique enough, that even this boat had not made a significant dent in her net worth. She could sail a long time yet before she'd have to think about money, if ever. She was the most winning woman on the world racing circuit. Sponsors, even the ones she'd jilted at the New York dock, would gladly line up at her least show of interest.

So, why had she sailed here to Gloucester of all places?

The night offered no clues. She fell asleep near midnight, marked by the half moon clearing the horizon to spread a ghostly glow across the thin cloud cover.

6

———

Morgan watched for her all day. Mary Elizabeth hadn't come to the beach. He'd know her walk in a heartbeat among the hundreds who strolled along the sand. Watching her walk away from him to dive into the sunset sea last night had anchored that firmly.

She walked as she had as a child, with a determination and an assuredness of direction as clear as a laser beam. The body had changed, very nicely, and the long flow of blonde hair trailed off her shoulders as it always had. But her walk had been stamped as clear as a thumbprint upon his artist's memory.

While she might be hidden, the boat remained— anchored close off the beach. Once or twice he though he spotted movement aboard but it was always gone before he could be sure.

Instead he focused on the sand. Romero caught up with him as he carved his way down and Morgan had to keep stopping to be sure of the image in his head. No, actually while he kept stopping to see if Mary had come ashore and to make sure she hadn't left.

Patricia had rebuilt the top tier of her sculpture and was only now beginning to carve. At first he'd thought she was also carving a sailboat, but soon the fin became clear. It was going to be an orca—he should have known. She loved her cetaceans. He wondered what it would be eating this time, as they almost always were. Seals, dolphins, even the occasional octopus. A tad grisly, but it gave it an immediacy that he knew the crowds always appreciated no matter how much they cringed at the realism of her fabulous technique.

For others, the high turrets of several fairy tale castles were coming into being. Those competitors were lucky Marcus wasn't here; his castles combined medieval battlements, luscious fantasy, and occasional Escheresque modern whimsy that occupied the mind long after the sand had fallen. He was the best casteller living as far as Morgan was concerned. He was also in Italy this week.

Maybe if he too had done castles, or any one thing consistently, he'd have a career like Marcus'. But he hadn't. Every sculpture was a unique creation ripped from who-knew-where. He knew where this one came from though.

In the other direction down the row, for he was near the middle, a leaping fish attempted to look airborne but instead looked quite scared. A Greek Parthenon two past that. A stepped Inca pyramid in which the roughness of stone and the details of climbing ivy were taking the simple structure to the next level. Perhaps too simple to win, but elegant nonetheless.

A newcomer was fated to doom as he worked to erect an Egyptian obelisk made of sand. There simply wasn't enough width below to support the height and angle he was carving. Not even a mix with a few parts of food-grade glue would hold it up. Morgan gave it a practiced assessment. It might make it until end of day, but the humidity was supposed to fall tonight and the obelisk would dry and be gone by morning. Too bad, it was pretty work right down to the chiseled look of the hieroglyphs.

On his own sculpture, he had two tiers to go, the last four feet of the fifteen. The sails towered a full story above him, looking truly as if they were racing across the sea.

He wished Mary was here to ask for her permission, but was also glad that she wasn't so that he didn't risk receiving a no.

Morgan built up a small section near the stern of the boat and began carving her hair caught in the wind.

7

———

Mary slipped ashore before the dawn to see the sculptures. She kept the wide-brimmed sunhat pulled low, she'd certainly missed it yesterday sitting so long in the sun and watching Morgan.

Today she'd be gone before they unlocked the gates and anyone arrived on the beach. Only a napping guard remained to ward off any vandals. The scattering of inevitable morning joggers on the hard sand marred the morning stillness. She'd be over the horizon before full sunrise, leaving this world behind for good.

The call yesterday had decided her. She'd up-anchor and head for Miami. It was time for a change and the timing couldn't have been better.

Most of the US Olympic team had already been training for months at the US Sailing Center on Biscayne Bay, but that didn't worry her. She was still carving her future, not protecting her past achievements. She'd slide in and simply outsail anyone who came after her.

They wanted her badly enough that she'd been able to

dictate the terms; they'd try each other on for thirty days and see what they thought. No harm no foul if she chose to sail away—though she assumed that she'd never be invited back if she did. If they decided she wasn't the winner they needed? Well, she wasn't worried about that.

It was time, *past* time for a change of pace. For two years she and the *Niles P.* had taken on the solo racing circuit all over the world. She hadn't done a full circumnavigation yet, and still didn't know if she really wanted to or if it was merely a new hurdle to check off some imaginary list. Time to join other sailors, hone her technique. Refresh her thinking.

But when she should have upped anchor and turned south, Mary hadn't. She'd been riveted all through yesterday, able to see the sails of her boat forming beneath Morgan's fast-moving hands. They rose from the fine white sand like the lovely racing boat the *Niles P.* was.

Morgan hadn't been visible for most of yesterday afternoon. He'd made quick work of carving the lower hull and echoing the clean lines of her boat. The rest of the day he'd spent working on the shore side of the sculpture. She knew this was the final day and that the judging was this evening, but she planned to be well out to sea and cruising south by then. She wasn't above having a private look; it was her boat after all.

Maybe she would carve him a note in a pile of discarded sand to wish him well. That too could wash away with the first rain. Then her past would be fully dissolved.

She slid her dinghy up on the dark sand, threw out a small four-pound Danforth lunch hook, and kicked its flukes into the sand to keep the anchor in place. Besides, she should really hike up to Jeff's Variety Deli or the grocery store and load up on some fresh supplies for the long sail south. It would be against the prevailing wind and current, summer was not the time to be sailing south opposite the flow of the Gulf Stream. But neither had it been the time of year to race a North Atlantic crossing—and she'd managed that nicely enough.

She put Miami at four days in ideal conditions, which this wasn't, and had told them to expect her in ten for tryouts. She'd make it in six. Maybe seven.

Mary appreciated the smooth lines of her sailboat rising from the sand as she approached Morgan's sculpture from the seaward side. He had carved neat waves all along the base to mask the inward curve of the hull where he'd needed a broader base for more support.

It was when she came around the other side that she went stock still.

Difficult to see in the low sunrise light driving in from the east, the landward side of the sculpture was in deepest shadow.

As her eyes adjusted, she made out the boat's skipper. Morgan hadn't used either the hunchback figure she'd mocked him with nor the recumbent mermaid she'd offered afterward.

Instead he'd taken the classic Gloucester fisherman, shrouded in his Sou'wester and clutching the ship's wheel and replaced it with *her*. Her hair coiled in tangled confusion at the strong wind of his imagination, some strands plastered across her cheeks. She faced the sea with...something.

Desperation or dismay would be most likely, but Morgan had made a different choice. He'd given her a half smile. Not as if she was ready to battle the sea, or was ever dumb enough to think such a thing was possible. A sailor *survived* the sea, never beat it. It was...

She wasn't sure.

Glancing at the time, she shrugged on her knapsack, followed the passage through the dunes, crossed the parking lot, the road beyond, and climbed the hill to the grocery store.

The beach parking lot attendant was already unlocking by the time she returned, but if she hurried, she'd be gone before the first cars had parked and unloaded.

Across the lot, through the low dunes on the rough boardwalk, and...Morgan was already there. His bicycle was tossed atop the pile of discarded plywood forms and his concentration was wholly on the sculpture.

He had a barber's lather brush in one hand, a tiny scraping tool little bigger than a scalpel in the other, and, in one corner of his mouth, a clear length of surgical tubing.

As she watched, he brushed at a strand of her rendered-in-sand hair, then blew a small blast of air through the surgical tube to remove the least bit of loosened sand. She didn't know how, but she could see the difference in the areas he'd gone over already. They were sharper in some way she couldn't discern. In a way that...brought her to life.

"What are you doing to me?" She hadn't meant to blurt it out that way.

Morgan took a careful step back from his sculpture before turning to look at her, the clear plastic tube clamped in his teeth like a writer might chew on a pen while thinking. "Good morning, Ms. Mary Elizabeth."

"Good morning, Captain Backward Pirate. What are you doing to me?" She waved a hand unsure if she was indicating his incredible attention to detail, the look on her statue's face that she still couldn't equate with her own, or something inside that she refused to think about.

"I'm shaping you in sand. I hope that's okay. You weren't around to ask, and you do have the most beautiful face, Mary."

"I can see that. That you're using my face. The latter part of that statement only makes me question your sanity. No. I meant—" But what did she mean? He saw her in a way that she'd never seen herself.

Again she studied the expression on her doppelgänger's features and didn't know what to make of it.

"You were always my ideal of beauty. I'd have known you anywhere."

She couldn't have picked Morgan out of a crowd. The small boy with the smart mouth that was always getting him in trouble was in no way reflected in this man before her. She knew the boy. The man? Not even a little. Yet the more she looked at her figure in sand, the more she thought that perhaps he knew more about her than she did herself.

"I'm sorry, it's really too late to change. I can try, but I don't think it will work. I should have—"

"It's okay, Master Pirate. It's okay," she cut off his rush of words. "It's just...weird seeing myself there in sand. Looking all..." She shrugged. "Maybe I spend too much time alone at sea. Using words? It's not something I do very often."

"You really race solo in that beast?"

"Mostly. Yes. The last two years exclusively. I'm going to be changing that soon."

He nodded sagely, as if he had a deeper wisdom, and turned back to continue his work. It was complete—to her unpracticed eye—with an entire day ahead of him. Yet every place he touched her likeness was better as he moved past it.

"Need a hand?" He asked without turning.

"A hand? I can carry my own groceries." Though she'd gone a little overboard and the pack was heavy. Vegetables, bread, cookies, as well as the more normal pasta and canned goods. There would also be a Jeff's Variety and Deli Italian Cold Cuts sub if she hadn't wolfed it down for breakfast on the walk back to the boat. She should have ordered two. That was a local taste she'd miss.

8

Mary Elizabeth Thomas was always a logical girl, Morgan mused, no surprise that she was still that way as a woman. He decided that the collar line of her Sou'wester should fall a little lower down her neck, she had a great neck. He selected a round-cornered rhombus Venetian plasterer's trowel from his tool bag, and reshaped the entire curve of the jacket. With an offset cupcake icer, he extended the hint of a curve made by her jugular vein, then blew air to clear the flaked-away sand.

A careful spritz of water, from a full foot back so the merest mist wetted the surface, and he studied the result. Yes, it was her.

"You've changed, and haven't," he didn't turn to look at her. It wasn't that he didn't need to—he didn't as she was so firmly fixed in his mind. It was that he didn't quite dare.

"Oh this should be good." And that hint of the old teasing tone they used to share was back.

He moved on to the shape of the Sou'wester where it would be plastered against her shoulder. "You still interpret everything in the most immediate way. *I have groceries, they're heavy, that must be what he's talking about.*

"You don't know me." But after a long moment he heard the knapsack hit the sand with a clank of cans.

"No, but I knew you. Closest thing I had to a friend, I studied you a lot. I don't think we can change that much." With her shoulder properly in place, he stepped back to study the angle of her arm as she gripped the wheel. He'd pedaled out to the tall bronze statue of the Gloucester fisherman along the Boulevard before sunrise this morning to make sure it was clearly fixed in his head. Did Mary see how much of that determination was in her as well?

"You remained the artistic boy following his own vision no matter what it drew down upon your head?"

He paused without turning.

"Sorry," she said quietly. "That came out sounding wrong. It was a skill I always admired in you. Your willingness to be yourself and to hell with all consequences."

And wasn't he paying the price now? The American medical system had caught them, stepping in to help only after Dad's cancer had wiped out all of Mom's and his own savings. Mom had died within weeks of Dad, the life had simply gone out of her. The house was gone to pay off the last of the debts. He now had a bicycle, his tools, and a spot on a buddy's couch.

He should have...he didn't know what. Saved more? Become a world-class cancer doctor to have found a miracle cure for Dad? Become a grief counselor who could have saved Mom?

Instead he carved sand.

A strange, ephemeral existence so easily erased by wind, rain, or simply time.

Morgan shook himself and did his best to return to the carving. If he won this one, he could afford to pay a little rent for his couch space, eke it out to the next job or competition. And then?

"The consequences can really suck."

9

———

Mary studied Morgan's back as he worked. His shoulders had slumped as he'd paused, slumped like Atlas' from holding up the world.

Then, somehow, when it looked as if it might crush him, he shrugged it off and returned to sculpting her. She watched for hours as he worked over every shape, going grain-by-grain—except her face. He never once touched that look on her sand-mirror's face. As if that alone was already perfect.

She sat on the sand leaning back against her pack. Others had arrived without her really noticing. The beach was crowded. The event manager had put up a line of stakes with orange tape from one to the next to keep the growing crowds from coming too close. She was one of the only non-sculptors inside the barrier.

The Day of the Dead figure was done. Its colors garish, almost painful to the eye in the morning light. The sculptor smoothed here and there, but that was all.

The Egyptian obelisk had collapsed in the night. The sculptor had stopped at the orange-tape border, stared at it for perhaps thirty seconds, then walked away without a word.

The castles were impressive in size, but they were simply castles. A gigantic school of leaping fish was wonderful in concept, but rough in execution. Still, very dramatic.

The best of the others was an arcing orca with a massive octopus in its jaws. The too-real, sand-brown tentacles stretched back along the orca, still fighting for purchase, struggling to do damage. It was dramatic and would be an easy winner.

If not for Morgan's sailboat. The level of precision and detail showed his mastery was beyond all of the others. Though that was only a piece of it.

No one could have missed that the boat of sand matched the one of fiberglass, aluminum, and Dacron moored offshore. Fewer, far fewer as she kept her sunhat pulled low, noted that she was the model for the skipper.

Instead, she could hear all of the whispered comments at the orange tape line close behind her that he'd captured the true spirit of Gloucester.

That unchanging face.

The statue had been a memorial back in 1923 on the three-hundredth anniversary of the founding of the city. *They that go down to the sea in ships.* In honor of the hundreds of fisherman who had lost their lives fishing from this port.

For a century since, that bronze skipper had stared out of the harbor, ready to fight the storm.

Battling, perhaps past reason, because that was simply what one did. She knew that place. When the storm wracked the boat. Double-reef on the main. Nothing but a small Number Four jib for a headsail. No autopilot could manage such chaos. Adjustments were made to each wave approach with the lone goal of protecting the boat. Nothing to do but survive the storm.

Grim determination. That was expression of the Gloucester Fisherman's Memorial.

But Morgan had given her lips the slightest hint of a smile. Little more than a Mona Lisa smile, yet it changed everything. *Bring it on!*

Not sailing alone in fevered grim determination. But also in...hope? Perhaps too strong a word. Maybe...possibility?

A covert glance showed that more and more people had come to gather opposite his sculpture and watch his finishing touches. A clear crowd favorite. Yet he remained oblivious to the attention, staying focused on making the perfect even better until she couldn't stand it any longer.

"Stop! Just...stop!"

10

———

Morgan felt as if all the strings that had kept his arms in motion were cut at once.

His hands dropped to his side. The tools slipped from his nerveless fingers to tumble upon the sand with soft plops. He spit out the short length of surgical tube.

Then his legs let go and he collapsed onto the sand beside Mary.

But he didn't need to turn to see her expression, her thoughts. They were writ so clear upon the sand before him. He knew this person better than he knew himself.

Yes, the memory of her had held him upright through many, and even grim, challenges. Seeing her dream floating offshore, manifested into reality through pure willpower had told him the rest. She too had persevered through her own joys and failures. A quick search on his phone that first night had shown the mark she had slashed across the yachting world.

Women didn't do that. Not to the old boys' club. Except Mary Elizabeth didn't compete "like a girl," she competed like a skipper. Like someone who was in perfect command of who she was.

Making that jibe with the woman he'd risen from the sea, not so unlike Botticelli's Venus, had been the true challenge. Finding that vision, that emotion—the tough competitor, competing with no one harder than she did with herself, had been the true challenge.

Not proud. Not afraid.

He knew he'd really achieved a life's goal when his hands had carved the face he couldn't put words or emotion to. Compared to the rest of the sculpture, it was the least polished but he hadn't dared touch it for fear of ruining the whole. Sitting now, looking up at her in the sand, he could see it was that *im*perfection that made it so powerful. That made it seem to leap forward into the world past all of the real-world elements of boat, sail, and storm. That made it shine in the sand.

"I've never done anything like this before."

"It's...incredible, Morgan. Really incredible."

He had to blink several times before he could break the hypnosis and turn to look at her. "Did you just call me by my first name?"

She scoffed. "I've done that a bunch of times."

He shook his head slowly. "Not even the first day we met at the beginning of grade school. I'd remember. You're the one who tagged me as the Backward Pirate the first day, I hadn't even heard of Sir Henry Morgan yet and you had already tagged me with him."

Now she was the one blinking hard. "I did?"

"Day One," he assured her.

"And is this what backward pirates do, make sailboats out of sand?" Her teases always made him want to laugh.

Would this time too, if the question hadn't been at the heart of everything.

"Up until now." He began gathering the tools that had landed about his feet, brushing them clean, and slipping them into his toolbelt. When she still didn't speak, he concentrated on digging the sand out from under his fingernails. It didn't matter how short he kept them; sand always found a way to wedge in.

"*Need a hand?*" she said almost dreamily when she finally spoke.

He didn't look up.

"What happened, Morgan?" Mary Elizabeth Thomas had never been stupid.

He tried to shrug it off but she wouldn't let him. So as the final afternoon wound down—he told her.

How he'd survived school by immersing himself in the art crowd, eventually learning enough taekwondo to defend himself physically and ignoring the rest. The death of his parents. The fact that he was starting over.

"If I win this—"

Mary scoffed at his *if*.

"It pays off the last of the medical debts. Maybe enough for a fresh start, though I'll be damned if I know at what."

"This?" she nodded toward his sculpture as if it was a worthy goal in and of itself. Only Dad and fellow maniacs like Romero ever believed that.

"Maybe. I like doing it. But I haven't done anything else —ever. Hell, Mary, you've raced all over the world. Except for an intense block of days sand castling here and there, I haven't been past Marblehead in years. In my life, I guess. With Mom and Dad no longer anchoring me here, I'm starting to look up at the horizon. And when I do..." he looked up.

She waited him out.

He waved a hand at her sailboat. "When I do look up, I see that gorgeous boat sailed by my favorite woman in the world, ready to leap into the future. What do I do? *That!*" He waved his hand at his sculpture in disgust. "I can take reality and make it mundane."

"You can take a dream and show it to others." Then her voice dropped to a whisper he could barely hear. "You showed it to me."

He could feel the time was growing short. The judges were gathering at the far end of the works. Mary was sitting against a knapsack of fresh supplies. She'd be gone by sunrise. She'd be gone if he so much as blinked. Somehow, he'd held her here one last day with his portrait of her, but that wouldn't hold. It was all carved in sand.

"*Need a hand?* you asked. Do you sail, Backward Morgan?"

"Almost every day since you left. Had a Laser and won most races down in Marblehead with her. Yet another thing I had to sell when Dad got sick. I was a fair foredeck hand on a J/24—other people's. Never quite put together having one myself."

The judges were drawing closer. They sounded like a good group, not rushing through the afternoon. Instead they spent time with each artist, making kind noises. Offering tips and occasionally commiseration where called for. When an entire castle turret splattered them with its abrupt collapse, they'd laughed and assured the sculptor that they'd be judging it on the pre-collapse state even though it wasn't quite five o'clock yet.

The tone for the contest was fun and success.

But what was the tone here at the base of his female mariner?

Again Mary was all whispers, "I received a phone call last night—"

"Crap!" He scrambled to his knees and crawled over to the stern of the sand boat.

"I—" she sounded like she was strangling on something. The judges were approaching Romero's sculpture, the last one before his.

He took the time for a single calming breath. Then he began carving faster than he ever had in his life.

Caught halfway to making an insane suggestion, Mary didn't know whether to be thrilled or annoyed at being cut off.

Morgan was back in his intense mode. Tools in either hand, surgical tube in his mouth, spray bottle close to hand.

The judges had slowed at Romero's to discuss coloring techniques, earning their own on-the-spot master class much to the interest of the watching crowd that had been moving down the line with them.

Still Morgan worked. Not frantically, but without a wasted thought or motion. Without so much as a *sorry* or a *hold on* to her.

He was still carving when the judges finished with Romero and came up to him. He ignored them as thoroughly as he ignored her.

From their vantage, they saw something that amused them. Their eyes flickering from the boat, to her image, to what he was carving into the stern. Then one of them focused on her and quickly whispered to the others. All three looked at her closely then nodded with knowing smiles. Yep, she'd been pegged as Morgan's model.

And still Morgan the backward pirate carved.

When at last he finished, he flopped from his squat to sit. But the judges had moved too close and, in sitting, he knocked two of them to the sand. The third one waved a hand to her to come look.

As she rose, the rest of the crowd began to murmur and point. She was going to have to murder Morgan. That worked, she supposed as he was a backward pirate and it was only appropriate for the damsel to do *him* in.

She circled until she stood staring at the name he'd carved into the back of the sand boat. *The Mariner* in an arc of perfectly chiseled letters above a smaller port of call, *The World.* And in between them, he'd added her form, stretched out in full mermaid pose.

It wasn't the fish tail or the overlong hair masking the obviously naked breasts that stopped her. It was the smile. It was the view of the *possible* that lay upon the features of the image of herself in sand gripping the wheel—but made certain. Made real.

He still sat with his butt on the sand, looking at her, not at the judges or what he'd done. Asking a simple question that was everything, *Need a hand?*

She'd sailed alone metaphorically and actually for most of her life. Somehow, for reasons beyond her understanding, Morgan Henry understood that about her.

It would be simple to call Florida. They wanted her on the team badly enough, she could convince them to give Morgan the same thirty-day tryout. She knew what it meant to be a frequent winner at Marblehead; that had been a hard climb for her as well.

Yes, there was the solo Laser class of racing at the

Olympics, she'd expected to excel in the women's division there. But there were also the 470s and the catamaran Nacra 17s requiring a mixed man-woman crew of two.

There were also deep-ocean races that called for a big boat like hers but allowed for a crew. Or perhaps she could give herself permission to simply stop now and then. Sail to Australia for a sand sculpting contest, it was less than two months away by boat, after all.

She didn't know what else Morgan Henry the Backward Pirate could see in her but he apparently liked whatever it was as his smile matched both hers and the hopeful mermaid carved in the sand.

SANTA AND THE PIRATE QUEEN

ABOUT THIS STORY

Against all bounds of common sense, Janine lands herself in charge of her yacht club's annual Christmas Potluck. Sailing the tricky course between a clean finish and a complete wreck, she desperately needs a rescue. Or perhaps it's time to set her own course.

Howie loves to sail but saving to buy his own boat takes time. He volunteers as crew when he can. And for the annual whirl of yacht club parties, he gate crashes as Santa.

When he sees one club has declared a pirate theme, he can't resist and goes in with full sails set.

But neither of them expect to find love in Santa's gift bag.

1

———————

The wind gusted past sixty knots out of the west-northwest. Not an issue from any other point of the compass, but WNW winds slid past the marina's breakwater, took a stroll down the lane between T and U docks, and hammered into slip T19.

Her slip.

Anything over forty-seven knots made her boat bob and weave like a drunk penguin.

"November storms suck!" Janine yelled at the boat. Ship's Captain Master Howl opened one eye, rolled onto his back and began to purr, forcing Janine to rub his furry black belly. Not as if she could do anything else. Her forty-one-foot Cheoy Lee sailboat, *Tārā*, twisted badly enough that she was far more likely to type *Gwko~* than *Help!* or *Sthj@* than *ARGH!* as the laptop slid one way and her fingers went the other.

Giving it up, she slapped the cover closed and tucked it into the drawer under the chart table. Scooping up Master Howl in her arms, Janine staggered forward—banging a shoulder against the starboard door to the head, almost dropping Master Howl as she crashed her hip against the cooktop in the portside galley, and finally shuffled fast enough to plummet into the starboard-most seat of C-shaped settee rather than plunging into the closet.

The settee was the oddest feature of the Cheoy Lee's design, but one she'd come to love. Most boats would have two sofa seats with some awkward arrangement to raise a table in the middle of the aisle when guests and meals were happening. Her boat had a circular sofa that could seat eight. The mouth of the C-shape opened to the stern to either side of where the mast punched through on its way to the keel. A fold-up table hung from the back of the mast.

She shuffled around the seat until the two of them were ensconced in the backmost position. This part of the seat could be folded aside to access the forward cabin, which she rarely used except for sail storage. Once seated on the centerline of the boat, the action felt much less violent, now no more than a gentle rocking. Books flopped side-to-side on the shelf with a gentle slap. Spice bottles rattled against each other in the galley. Miscellaneous gear clanked to one side then another in the various storage cubbies. And though she couldn't hear the water sloshing about in the bilge, she could hear the pump engage and shut down as it was alternately submerged and exposed with the rolling of the boat.

All the sounds of home. Then a blast of rain and hail pounded on the deck over her head, drumming like an all-percussion marching band.

"Gonna be a long night, Master Howl."

He answered with an orca-sized yawn as befit his black coat and white chest patch. Though his hair fell more into the shaggy category than the sleek and dangerous one.

He *had* been a howler as a kitten but age had mellowed him. It was now far easier to picture him snoozing in a rope coil, sipping a White Russian (without the vodka or Kahlúa diluting the cream, of course), and occasionally rousing himself to batter his catnip toy crew into submission. It made him the perfect ship's captain. Though he still did occasionally give full voice to his discontent—especially if his dinner was more than three seconds late. He considered her ignoring that while navigating tricky archipelago passages to be grounds for mutiny. She had taught him quickly enough that batting her with his claws out counted as a gross breach of the ship's articles under which she served.

Of course it was better than being saddled with a dog. She'd trust Joshua Slocum on that point. On sailing the first solo circumnavigation of the globe in the 1890s, he'd considered taking on a local to help him pass through the Strait of Magellan. But the man had insisted that no one in their right mind would attempt that passage without a *doog* on board. Per his book *Sailing Alone Around the World*, Slocum *drew the line at dogs*. Janine had cleaved to that advice and never regretted her decision to do so.

Here, at the centerline with a warm cat in her arms, and the boat rocking side-to-side like the perfect cradle for a grown woman, she wanted to fall asleep. She really did. She tried.

Master Howl succeeded easily enough.

But her? Oh no! Tomorrow was *her* day and it wouldn't stop churning up a turbulent wake in her head.

With kind words and the hints of how much fun it would be, the secretary-general of the local yacht club had suckered her into organizing the annual Christmas Sailor's Potluck. A crime for which she'd never forgive him.

The reality had no relation to the purported ease and fun.

The other volunteers' expectations were that they could have everything exactly their way, that it was fully under their control, and that the louder they protested the more likely they would succeed.

However, Janine had been sailing far too long to be fooled. Everyone who had ever skippered a boat, even an eight-foot rubber dinghy, would gladly don a t-shirt declaring *I'm the Captain so, of course, I'm right!* She tried not to wince at the one in her own collection stating *I'm the Captain. Rule #1: The Captain is always right. Rule #2: Any questions? See Rule #1.*

Organizing a potluck should be merely sending out a few fun invites and reminders. A little bit of dish coordination so that not *everyone* brings a package of QFC chocolate chip cookies, and make up a few fun door prizes.

Except Georgina Anne wanted there to be fixed seating and a size limit.

Michael wanted to turn it into a fifty-dollar-a-head fundraiser (that Janine was sure was actually to keep the riff-raff like herself out but that Georgina Anne took personally).

Bethany had organized a decorating committee with her two BFFs, and they'd wanted a committed budget several times the yacht club's annual membership fee.

This wasn't the Seattle Yacht Club costing tens of thousands of dollars with thirty-six-month payment plans (for those in need). Nor was it the Sloop Tavern Yacht Club with a ninety-dollar fee, which also registered your boat for all of their races. She'd chosen one that cost in the hundreds —after having broken up with the head barman at the Sloop, which had definitely cancelled her prior membership there. Danny had been cool about it, but not the patrons.

The Lakefront Yacht Club landed in the casual zone between the two. A little upscale from the guys chugging pints at the start of a race no matter what the hour. It made for a nice change. Except the LYC also gathered all of the wannabes who the Seattle Yacht Club would never allow on their clubhouse verandah much less as members. And the worst of the lot had harangued her hourly on every social media platform known to womankind.

Finally sick of them all, she'd issued the invite to the full membership for the Annual Christmas *Pirate's* Potluck, set a suggested door price of a wrapped present for a homeless kid, and called it done. Once out, no one had the balls to take it back. When Bethany and her BFFs had attempted to vote her out, she'd invoked the *I'm-the-Captain* rule. Finally, the club's secretary-general had backed her up over Bethany's protests with a simple e-mail: *Janine's the organizer.* Three whole words from a man who typically communicated in story-length volumes.

Tomorrow would either be immense fun. Or—

"Worst they can do is keelhaul me, right, Master Howl?"

On a particularly rough buck of the boat, her cat rolled out of her arms to plop into her lap, more like a beanbag than a cat with an actual skeleton somewhere beneath all that fur.

Janine sighed and began beating the back of her head against the partition that separated the settee from the forward stateroom. Not hard enough to knock herself out, though the thought did come to mind.

2

Howie Liebermann loved Christmas. Or at least the Christmas season. Mom loved having the annual *Hanukkah bush* in the living room. Dad always turned surly for a week or so after its arrival before caving in. It was hard to blame him. Each year he caught hell from Grandma when she visited, which seemed unfair as Jews didn't go in for the whole Hell thing—more of a Limbo-like retraining center for souls destined to enter the Garden of Eden on high.

Howie and his two sisters could always count on the worst presents under the Menorah. How many wooden dreidels and cheap milk chocolate wrapped in gold foil did three kids need after all? Grandma's Fifth Night gelt always eased the pain a little. The five-dollar *fortune* they'd received as little kids had never crossed twenty even in the lean college years. She paid their tuitions—her and Grandpa's sewing machine business had been very successful—but never more than a twenty on Fifth Night. The best presents always landed *under* the Hanukkah bush —which they had trimmed with twinkle lights and eclectic ornaments. Presents that just happened to be opened on December 25th, though nothing from Grandma, of course.

That wasn't why he loved Christmas.

His passion for the holiday season had sprung into being when he'd escaped Brooklyn under the impetus of a cool job and cruised into Seattle's land of year-round sailing.

And the best part about Christmas here was definitely the great sailing parties and races. The Seattle Yacht Club Championships close before Halloween, typically coincident with the Sloop Tavern's Great Pumpkin Race at the other end of the spectrum. The Turkey Bowl race that the Corinthian Yacht Club on the Friday after Thanksgiving. Again, the Sloop's Dark & Stormy Christmas Light Cruise (and inevitable after-party). All the nights with parades of Christmas boats along different sections of Seattle's vast waterfronts were illumination spectacles.

And every club had an annual Christmas potluck.

Howie had never joined any of the clubs, though he'd enjoyed the round of *Introduction* dinners every club offered as they sought new members. Instead, he'd made a small name for himself on the local race circuits as on-call crew when a boat came up a person short.

He learned that it was a *thing* two years ago while hanging out at Fremont Brewing's Urban Beer Garden after a long day cutting code at Adobe. Their offices commanded the waterfront by the Fremont drawbridge.

At the next table, a couple were fighting about whose turn it was to helm the boat in that night's race. Watching the summertime Tuesday Duck Dodge evening races out on Lake Union in the heart of Seattle was fun. But he'd never given any thought to being aboard, until the guy had stormed off and the woman looked around the bar like a lost soul. Short, cute, and curvy, they'd dated long enough for him to learn the basics of sailing and have a good laugh together. She let him and other volunteers crew every position, except the helm—that was hers alone now that she'd canned the fiancé.

Howie had quickly learned to read the local racing calendars and started making a few educated guesses. The Fremont Brewery or Duke's on Tuesday afternoons led to Duck Dodge slots. The bar at Ray's Boathouse the night before a race out of Shilshole turned out to be a great place to be picked up as last-minute crew. Laurelhurst had too much money to ever consider wanting crew like him, but Anthony's Homeport along the Kirkland waterfront was a consistent winner.

There were now a score of boat skippers with his number on speed dial. Two, even three races a week came his way almost year round. He'd never spent a dollar past his bar tab, one pint and an appetizer limit unless some winning captain was buying for the crew. There'd been no need to join any of the yacht clubs.

Except for missing the Christmas parties.

Despite his initial introduction, sailing women were in a special class all their own—rare. Men dominated the sport. Howie soon learned, however, that grown-daughters-of came out of the woodwork at special moments...like Christmas parties.

But he had to adhere to his policy of minimal expense. He was only about halfway to affording his own boat big enough to live aboard but fast enough to be fun. Or maybe even rigged for the ultimate: going deep sea. Circumnavigating. Hard to imagine but it sounded very cool. Until then? He'd stay focused on hitting those great holiday parties.

He'd built enough connections to enough different boats

that he always heard about the various parties. This being the self-proclaimed sailing capital of the US of A, there were a lot of them. Between Halloween and the end of the Christmas boat parades on December 23rd was in many ways the peak of the sailing season—or at least the *social* sailing season.

But finding a date, even on a one-evening basis to attend a party, was tricky because the sailing women were so rare.

Then the great idea came. Who could turn away a gate-crashing Santa, even one with a Brooklyn-Jew accent?

3

———————

Janine surveyed the yacht club decorations. Thank God last night's storm had played itself out, which would be a boon for attendance. She so didn't want to be the person who organized a party and no one came. From the crackling fire at one end of the hall to the giant Christmas tree at the other, it was beautiful.

"This is amazing! Great job!" Janine had to give credit where credit was due.

Bethany and her pair of BFFs offered her thankful smiles that didn't reach their steel-like eyes, but they *had* done well. And it had cost the club only fifty dollars.

In keeping with her Pirate's Christmas theme, the Queen Bethany Trio scrounged among the membership for old manila lines, wooden block-and-tackle, battered wooden chests, and the like. The tables, that Janine had insisted be set up in long communal-style rows over Georgina Anne's protests, were scattered with well-worn seafaring paraphernalia. The QBT had also raided various long-grown-children's toy boxes; rubber swords and daggers had been strewn about as well. Bethany had found nautical-chart paper tablecloths to spread along the tables, which had cost the fifty dollars and were sure to be conversation starters with any sailor.

Janine's personal playlist—of mixed sea shanties by the Cornish Fisherman's Friends group and Christmas carols—lent a cheery background.

Georgina Anne and Michael had eschewed festive wear beyond very conservative Christmas sweaters.

But not to be outdone by Janine's chosen theme, the QBT wore matching pirate maiden costumes that included high leather boots, alarmingly short skirts, and seriously low-cut bodices. Bandanas side-knotted as headbands allowed their latest hair styles to be on display while adding to the piratical air.

Courtesy of a brief fling several years ago that had overlapped Halloween, Janine possessed full Elizabeth Swann attire. Keira Knightley had rocked it in *Pirates of the Caribbean,* and their builds were similar enough that Janine had gone all in when putting it together—right down to the sheathed long sword dangling from a well-worn broad leather strap. Unsure why she could never throw it out, especially when space was always such a premium on a sailboat, she now knew. Without a word, simply by standing beside them, it changed the Queen Bethany Trio from sexy pirate maidens to cheap working girls in a pirate bar.

The fact was not lost on the BFFs, though Bethany pretended not to care. Of course, rumor said that Bethany was searching for a new *captain* for her personal boat, having divorced the second (or perhaps third) one two months ago. She appeared fully prepared to leverage all that the costume implied at the least hint of a major checking account.

Oddly, this was something relatively easy to assess in the

boating community. Finding out the size and make of a person's sailboat, a natural conversation starter in a yachting club, quickly separated the pretenders and the wannabes from the truly affluent. A C&C 27 earned a scoff at best, though a J24 might command a little respect as it was a racer rather than a wallowing daysailer. Anything over fifty feet commanded attention. Her 41-foot boat floated in the murky middle ground, though it being a Cheoy Lee did earn her more attention than a longer Gulfstar or Cal might.

By the time of the official start of the potluck, the hall was already half full—a good turnout. About half had taken her challenge with costumes ranging from a simple bandana to a few other kits better than the QBT. Too bad she was judging the best costume competition, as so far she would be an easy win.

Her top choice so far was a family who had dressed as space pirates with obviously recycled astronaut Halloween costumes. They weren't incredible but the family absolutely owned it, especially the five-year-old girl brandishing her kid-sized red light saber.

Steaming pots and great platters of food soon had the buffet table groaning under the weight. Three sets of Swedish meatballs, several lasagnas, salads in every variety from Asian noodle to orange-cranberry. Two whole sides of salmon were sufficiently massive that even a concerted attack didn't kill them off until past the first hour. Not a single Jell-O salad—a staple of her Iowan youth—reared its ugly head.

The dessert table was like a light show: blueberry cobbler, a great sheet of golden baklava, the round eyes of orange pumpkin and lemon-yellow meringue pies were interspersed with M&M oatmeal cookies larger than her hand with the fingers spread.

Yet Janine could feel the change like a good skipper reading the winds before they wholly shifted and left your boat stranded on the wrong side of the course.

Second helpings tapered off. The dessert buffet slightly resembled the docks after a fish-cleaning session. An hour in and the event showed the first signs of fading. It was too early to start on the door prizes. The Spring Fling had revealed that this wasn't much of a dancing crowd. She cursed herself for not thinking up any games, probably because she'd always hated them when someone else did.

This evening was on the verge of winding down long before she was ready, considering all the effort and pain she'd put into the event. Desperate enough to approach the Queen Bethany Trio? Sadly, yes.

But when she went looking for them, she could only find the two BFFs.

"She's showing her boat to someone." The BFFs' shared look said that she wouldn't be back anytime soon. The Solaris 40 might be a foot shorter than her Cheoy Lee 41, but the interior was pure luxury. Bethany and her latest target might not resurface for days.

The BFFs were far more tolerable on their own, but neither had any brilliant ideas to keep the party going either.

Maybe she should bow to the inevitable and start the door prizes early. Of course, with her luck, she'd then be accused of cutting short such a lovely evening. It was the no-win scenario with Captain Jack Sparrow nowhere in sight to rescue her. If she—

"Merry Christmas, ye blaggards!" The shout sliced through every conversation and focused all attention on the door.

4

—————

"Heya! Heya! Heya! Can Santa make an entrance or what?"

It earned him a polite round of applause. Kinda middle ground. Not the polite patter from the Medina Yachters nor the round of cheers and a beer thudded on the bar before him at the Sloop Tavern.

He jumped up onto a table, brandishing the sword that he'd spiral wound with red-and-white electrical tape.

"Arrrr! Come on people. Give Pirate Santa a proper arrr. ARRR!"

The response, especially from the kids and their families, improved by several levels. His little sister Stacey had been hyped on Broadway since seeing *The Lion King* at age six. She'd rarely been the lead in any school play, but she *always* nailed the scene-stealing comic relief. Good enough that this year Yale Drama gave her a major scholarship. For this event, he'd channel Stacey.

Howie flourished the hook clamped over his left hand. He'd picked it up at a local costume shop along with the sword, see-through eye patch, and tricorn hat. Though he'd never been *Pirate* Santa before, he couldn't resist the challenge when a buddy had forwarded him a copy of the invitation.

"ARRR!" he roared out again and the kids ate it up.

As he swashbuckled down the table, people yanked empty plates and glasses out of the way.

"So, who here has been a good lad or lassie—and who's been baaaad?"

A small voice popped up on cue. "I've been good," a pint-sized pirate with a raggedy shirt, a bandana, and an eyepatch flipped up.

"Good?" Howie blustered. "*Good?*"

He tucked his sword away and reached down to lift the little boy onto the table.

"I oughter make ya walk the gangplank. Less'n you was a-sayin' you were a good *pirate*." He'd lost the kid, so Howie helped him out. "You been a good *pirate* for Pirate Santa, young lad?"

His sister had taught him that one of the keys was to dress the part. So, he'd done the full Santa fat suit and beard, and layered on the pirate with eyepatch, tricorn hat that he'd spray-painted bright red, and latex-makeup scars on the bits of cheek and forehead that showed. The other key, she'd insisted was to ham it up and never break character. So, he laid on the Brooklyn accent, the one he'd done his best to leave behind along with his youth, as thick as a Katz's pastrami on rye and dove into the pirate role.

"Yes, Pirate Santa."

"Well done, lad!" He unslung the red gift bag he'd been wearing on a wide leather strap. Peeking inside, he found a Matchbox fire engine, the full ladder truck with the pivot in the middle, and handed it over. In moments, the pirate-in-training was once again in his chair, racing his new engine around the plate holding the last few bites of an apple pie.

"Har! Har! Har! Merry Christmas, lad!"

5

Janine slid over to stand by Georgina Ann and Michael. Now there was a match made in hell. Maybe she should push them together simply for the sheer spectacle. Of course, what if it worked? The vision dancing in her head of miniature versions of these two ruthlessly organizing the world was enough to stop the thought.

"Okay. Who hired the Pirate Santa from Brooklyn?"

They both shrugged. "We thought you did."

"It *is* rather crass," Georgina Ann continued. "Hadn't you already made a sufficient mockery of the event as it is?"

Michael was nodding his agreement.

"Gods, you two *do* belong together."

"We what?" they said in unison. Then they both looked at her before turning to inspect each other.

Crap! Now she really had unleashed the Christmas Gorgon or Hydra or whatever mythical monster it was that got released at Christmas.

Well, it *was* her event. Which meant whatever happened was up to her.

She moved up to Santa who'd returned to floor level as

he dug deep into his bag for a little girl.

"Ah!" he spotted her. "Santa's Pirate Elf just when I needed her. Sit. Sit." He pointed at the floor.

Caught unawares, Janine sat cross-legged on the floor, placing her eye-to-eye with the little girl.

Santa fished out a stethoscope.

"Put these in your ears," he instructed the little girl as he helped her. "And you'll hear something amazing."

He handed the business end to Janine. Without any hint of risqué, the V-neck of her blouse still opened enough for her to place the pickup close above her left breast.

The girl's eyes shot wide.

"You can listen to anyone's heart," the Pirate Santa told her.

"Even Mr. Tom's?" she asked in an overloud voice.

He tickled the side of her ribs with the tip of his plastic hook. "When ye get home, lass, listen right there, just behind Mr. Tom's front leg on either side. And try right here on his throat," the hook touched the side of Janine's throat, "when he starts to purr. Do you purr?"

Janine hadn't expected the last to be addressed to her.

Snagging her wrist with his hook, he moved the stethoscope from above her breast to beside her throat.

She pressed the pickup there and did her best to purr.

The girl giggled in delight. "You don't sound nothing like Mr. Tom." Then the shyness kicked in. She leaned in to whisper to the man in the well-padded red-and-white suit that was at least as high quality as her own pirate outfit. "Thank you, Santa." The girl scurried away, clutching her stethoscope tightly to her chest.

"I hope she has a patient cat," Pirate Santa appeared to be grinning behind the fake white beard.

"Who—" But her attempt to ask who he was, and each

subsequent attempt after that was cut off by the arrival of another child. He soon had a waiting crowd.

Each time, he listened carefully to them, asking questions. Then he'd fish around in his bag. Nothing was wrapped, nor was any of it new. Some showed signs of repair, touched-up paint and so on. But each gift delighted its recipient.

"How—"

She was as unsuccessful with that question as *Who*.

But during the quiet in-between moments, Santa explained. "Pirate Santa hits the thrift stores. Picks over the toy sections—"

"And the doctor ones," she interjected, realizing that the girl now owned a genuine stethoscope, not some imitation that would break before she could listen to her cat's heart.

"Sure. Marine stuff, farmer, chef—though no knives. Whatever comes to hand. Fix it up and give them away. It's a good goof, all in fun, dat fer sure. Pirate Santa and his pirate elf," he offered her a broad wink, "take care of his wee crewmates, dat's all o' the game." Only a lone eye was clearly visible, and one of the fake scars tugged the wink askew.

She'd swear that his Brooklyn accent grew thicker the longer she stayed near him. Janine was about to fade away, though not too far as he remained an unknown, when she caught onto the pattern of the gifts. Boys wanted the little cars and trucks along with the occasional action figures. For the girls, there were a few dolls, but most received a next-level gift like the stethoscope, a small hand telescope, or a children's book of knot-tying with a length of line. One of the older girls received a scientific calculator complete with a printed-off copy of the instruction manual.

That was what kept her closer than merely keeping an eye on him.

6

———

Howie had been following a routine that he'd honed a dozen or more times with great success. Though he'd never had an elf assistant before, especially not one who looked so incredible. At her first attempt to slip away, he placed the next little kid in her lap to keep her in place.

Long and sleek. Thick hair, the chocolatey brown of Santa's reindeer, flowed down over her shoulders and offered a glorious distraction. The low brim of her black tricorn hat shaded her eyes so that he couldn't see their color. And dressed in a costume that looked like it was straight out of the 1700s. She was utterly astonishing. Exactly the woman any pirate king would want by his side to make him the envy of all far and wide.

He set himself up on a chair on one of the tables and had her assisting *Those who sought an audience with Pirate Santa* to step up onto *Pirate Santa's throne*. She had the poise and build of a dancer, but demonstrated a surprising strength when handling even the stoutest boy or girl—a sailing pirate's strength for sure.

From up here, he could also judge the ebb and flow of

the room. He could usually sustain this game for ten or fifteen minutes. It was over half an hour before he finally closed his bag for the last time. Then he stood and bowed to the four corners of the room, honoring the four winds. The applause was almost a roar, his best yet. He could see why his sister was so hyped on it, even if he never wanted to do it out of a Santa—or a Pirate Santa—suit.

Then he reached out a hand toward the lovely elf. Not down, but coaxing her up to stand on the table beside him.

Her blush shot bright, but she stepped on a wobbly chair with perfect surety and joined him aloft.

Then he took her hand, raised their joined grasp high, then swung it down. Only a bit off the cue, she took the indication to bow. The applause continued.

As it died away, he called out, "Santa sees there's still plenty o' fine desserts awaitin'. What kind of a pirate crew are ye to be leaving such vittles laying about?" It earned a laugh and turned the crowd's attention back to the buffet line.

The elf retrieved her hand and jumped lightly down from the table. But she didn't walk away. Instead, she held the chair steady for him. He was far less graceful in his heavy boots, fat suit, and a hook for a left hand.

"Party crasher?" she asked from mere inches away once he stood again on *terra firma*. Her eyes were the color of a darkening sky, but he didn't see any storm brewing there.

"What else would ye expect from a Pirate Santa?"

"Far less than this one has earned tonight." She kissed him on the cheek above his white beard but below the latex scar that was squinting up his exposed eye—a mistake he'd never make again as it was seriously annoying.

By the end of the evening, Howie knew several things.

First, the elfin pirate had almost no skills with people.

She was as forthright as her pirate attire suggested. While she didn't offend, she was crap at superficial chit-chat. He recognized it as a trait they absolutely shared.

Second, she was organized enough to lead an entire pirate rabble to victory. The whole evening finished smoothly. Including the family of space pirates winning best group costume and a gift certificate to the Museum of Science.

Third, he remained his usual awkward real-life self despite being the Pirate Santa. He departed well-fed and thanked—without discovering her name or asking for her phone number.

Fourth, he was completely gone on the woman who had set a whole new standard for attractive piratical elves.

7

———

The Christmas Ship Parade of Boats was always a tricky challenge. Tourists paid top dollar to ride on the Argosy tour boat with fine cocktails, appetizers, and a caroling choir. No self-respecting Seattle boat skipper would be caught dead on such a cruise—or paying that much money for a ninety-minute outing.

However, it was the lead ship on the final night of the parade of boats dressed up in Christmas lights. On evenings throughout December, there were parades along different sections of Seattle's waterfront—something the city boasted a lot of. But December 23rd counted as the big one and she'd hate to miss it.

Janine had sailed every parade this year, and after going to so much trouble dressing up *Tārā*, she'd hate missing the final one. But her normal call-up crew felt that their office Christmas party was more important. She hoped that they told the truth about having to put in an appearance, rather than what she suspected—that they'd have more fun at their office than with her. Personally, she was always happiest alone on her boat.

She could single-hand *Tārā* in all conditions except for the busiest of races. But passing solo through the Ballard Locks was just begging for trouble. She moored at Shilshole Marina on Puget Sound, and tonight's cruise was along the Lake Union waterfront, five miles and one tricky set of locks away.

A few calls up and down the docks to the other liveaboards revealed they were having similar crew problems. Alice and Jake gave her a number to try. *He's a good hand, dead reliable. Decent guy.*

Her excitement about inviting a strange guy onto her boat for a six-hour cruise ranked mighty low. But when, six calls later, Quint gave her the same number, she caved.

A couple quick texts and she had her crew, for better or worse.

At T dock, pinged into her phone.

Janine glared at the text, then ponytailed her hair under her hoodie and pulled on a windbreaker. It was a good night, calm and dead clear, which meant chilly headed for downright cold. Sure enough, by the time she reached the head of the dock to open the security gate, she had to snug down the hoodie and was wishing for a mug of hot chocolate.

Though he was silhouetted by the parking lot lights behind him, the guy on the other side of the wire mesh didn't look dangerous. His height was all she could really tell, a few inches over hers. A cable-knit orange wool hat was tugged down to his eyebrows. A multi-colored scarf around his neck, and the heavy jacket said he knew what he was getting into. He was carrying a satchel.

"What have you got there?"

"My standard kit, though I hope I don't need it tonight: inflatable life vest, slicks, and a change of clothes."

"Okay." She opened the gate.

"There's also a dozen cookies from Dahlia Bakery in Belltown."

"You're hired."

He had a good laugh. Down at Slip T19 he came to a halt. "Is this a Cheoy Lee?"

"The 41." Janine was more than a little charmed. It was unusual enough that not many could pick one out of a crowd. "Her name is *Tārā*." She liked the way he scanned the boat. Not wide-eyed neophyte, but rather pausing only briefly as he cataloged the deck layout, line paths, and tiedowns.

"You don't strike me as the sort to be burning down the South."

Everyone always assumed that her boat was named for Scarlett's plantation in *Gone with the Wind*. Even if they saw the odd spelling, which this guy couldn't without going to the stern and bending down to look.

"Uh, I never got your name."

"Howie."

"Hi, I'm Janine. Thanks for lending a hand tonight."

"Always glad of a chance to cruise in the Christmas parades." He tossed his bag inside the lifelines.

She hopped aboard. "*Tārā* was a female Buddha or a bodhisattva, depending on who you talk to. She's the Mother of Liberation. Success in work and achievements also fall under her purview." She started the engine.

"Cool! Liberation from the hum-drum life. I like it." Howie caught the end of the spring line after she untied it, flipped it off the dock cleat and tossed it aboard forward in a neat coil. Without needing any prompting, he untied the stern line, left a loop over the dock cleat, and handed her the loose end. That would let her keep the boat in place until she was actively backing out of the slip. Finally he undid the bow line and stood ready to walk the boat out.

No questioning his familiarity with proper line work.

In minutes they were sliding through the night waters. He clipped the safety lines securely, then cleared the rubber bumpers that had dangled off the side between the boat and the dock. He continued until he'd dressed all the lines as neatly as she always did.

After snagging his bag, he hesitated at the head of the companionway down into the boat.

She waved him ahead as she navigated her way along the back of the Shilshole breakwater. Manners too. Who was this guy?

8

Howie didn't want Janine to think he was snooping; the woman came across as seriously serious. He'd intended to toss his bag on a bunk and return to the deck immediately, but the interior required a good long look.

She was no simple daysailer—neither the woman nor the boat.

There were obvious signs that not only did Janine live aboard, but that her boat was capable of far more serious adventures than a parade of Christmas lights. The instruments at the chart were top quality gear. Not merely an ICOM two-way, but also a handheld and a satellite radio. The GPS and navigation equipment was sufficiently impressive that he'd want a good long spell with the instruction manual before approaching it.

And the interior. Janine was a very practical woman. There were only hints here and there as to the owner's gender. But she had a fantastic physical library of the great mariners from Bligh to Chichester. There were also travel guides that appeared to include most major countries with a coastline. A slim set of volumes about Arctic and Antarctic exploration were particularly intriguing.

Too long below, though the thoroughly efficient and comfortable interior tempted him to linger, he turned to ascend the ladder to the deck.

Except his way was blocked. Sitting there at the base of the ladder, a large black-and-white cat regarded him suspiciously.

"What's his or her name?" he called up to Janine loudly enough to be heard over the engine rumble as he knelt to let the cat sniff his hand.

"He. Ship's Captain Master Howl. Be sure to salute."

He glanced up the ladder at her. What little of her face he could see between the hoodie and the darkness showed no sign she was joking. So, he knelt as straight as he could, then saluted sharply before reaching out to pet him. The cat had a ready purr.

Howie scooped him up and carried Master Howl up to join his mistress above decks.

"Now you're spoiling him rotten." She showed the first hint of humor since his arrival.

"And you don't? You made him ship's captain."

"Oh no, he did that on his own. I merely bowed to the inevitable. Here, take the wheel." And she simply walked away from him.

In all his sailing, it was the one thing he did the very least—as in never. It was part of how he'd fit into every crew, by never going for the wheel or tiller.

She disappeared below.

The steel wheel radiated cold against his palms, cold enough it almost burned. But he didn't dare let go to fish out his gloves. Instead, he held on for dear life and did his best to stay on track for the opening at the south end of Shilshole and the turn into Salmon Bay and the locks.

Foolishly trusting him, Janine stayed below forever—at least a minute, perhaps two. Other boats were coming out of darkened docks. Picking their running lights out of their extravagant Christmas finery was tricky.

Then she must have thrown a breaker and the *Tārā's* lights blinked on. Which was a massive understatement. The boat glittered with a galaxy of multi-colored lights. After that, everyone stayed out of his way as if he was Neptune, God of the Sea.

She finally reappeared, only to set down a pair of bowls on the floor of the cockpit. Master Howl thumped down from the seat he'd been lounging on and began eating his dinner.

Then Janine was back out of sight, reappearing only to set out a big thermos, then two mugs, and finally his box of cookies.

When she returned to the deck, she didn't take the wheel. Instead, she sat on one of the side seats and filled the two thermal travel mugs from the thermos.

"Hope hot chocolate's okay. I can't drink coffee past the first cup of the morning or I end up more jittery than Master Howl." As her cat seemed more likely to yawn than jitter, he wasn't terribly worried.

"Hot chocolate born and bred." He accepted the mug and managed the turn into Salmon Bay without crashing her boat into a channel buoy. A minor triumph in his opinion.

He could feel her eyes on him. "What's wrong?"

"I've never taken the helm before."

"Never? Why?"

He shrugged, though that probably didn't show through his heavy parka. "Earned my first ride as crew because of a couple fighting over control of the helm while they were still ashore. Figured my best way to keep sailing was to keep my hands off."

"But the rest of it?" She waved a gloved hand at the rest of the boat.

"A hundred and thirty-seven races from winch grinder to foredeck sail handler."

"Over hard right!" She snapped out.

He didn't see a reason but wasn't going to mess with that tone. He looked right to make sure no one was in the channel beside him and turned the wheel to starboard.

"Spin it! All the way!"

So he did through two full turns until the wheel hit a stop with a solid *thunk!* he could feel through his palms. The boat turned like it was dancing.

"Back the other way!"

He spun back to port, four turns until the wheel thunked against the other stop. The boat spun with equal agility in the other direction.

"Settle straight up the channel," her voice turned utterly patient.

She sat in silence as he tried but overcorrected one way and then the other before he found the center position again *and* had them headed in the right direction.

"That gives you a beginning feel for how she handles, agile without being twitchy."

And that set the tone for the evening.

She handled lines, but never touched the wheel or the engine controls. Instead, she offered clear, precise instructions on boat handling and then explained what he was feeling as he did so.

"Put the engine in neutral and feel how she coasts.

Twelve-six beam on a forty-one-foot hull weighing twelve tons fully loaded, she glides longer than you'd expect. Skeg keel, so if you nudge it into reverse, she only walks a little to the left."

He put it into reverse and, as they slowed, the bow did indeed swing to the left, but was easily corrected with a light turn of the wheel.

9

———

Twenty-two feet up through the busiest set of locks in the entire US, she kept a hawk eye on Howie, ready to leap in at the least provocation. But he tended to under- rather than over-control, which was a pleasant change and avoided the most common mistakes.

He learned incredibly quickly. It made sense once she thought about it. She typically set neophyte friends at the helm to get a feel for a boat. It was strange to have someone who was an experienced sailor in every way *except* steering.

Howie's attempts to relinquish control tapered off as he became more and more used to how the boat reacted. In her early days, she'd had to fight for even moments at a boat's helm, until she was so fed up that she'd bought her own. Janine had long ago sworn that she'd never be one of *those* skippers.

And if she were to take Howie at his word, he wasn't one of those control-freak-effing-asshole guys either.

They slid along the Washington Ship Canal in the company of the other eight boats that had been in their same lift through the locks. Others were joining them from the commercial yards to either side of the passage.

As they emerged into Lake Union, Howie lost all control. She didn't take the helm away from him, but did stretch out a foot without disturbing Master Howl in her lap and nudged the throttle back to idle.

"Holy shit!"

She could only smile. There were some experiences he clearly hadn't had. The various boat parades typically included twenty boats. This final-night gathering on Lake Union, in the northern heart of Seattle downtown, was an outright extravaganza.

Argosy Cruises had all three of their big tourist boats out and lit up like birthday cakes. Several boats in the hundred-foot-plus class floated like pylons in the middle of the lake for the other boats to swirl around. Powerboats abounded, from tiny skiffs to luxury yachts.

Sailboats stood out clearly because most had a string of lights that traced from the stern, up the mast's backstay to the peak, then down the forestay to the bow. Others enhanced that with a string of lights down the mast so that it looked as if their sails were up with edges alight.

Not quite sure why, Janine had gone a little crazy this year. She'd run lights up every shroud and sidestay, and wound around the main boom. More lights outlined the edge where deck met hull and others traced the top of the cabin. She'd done it all with colored LED twinkle lights so the cockpit itself remained shrouded in near darkness, but *Tārā* glittered.

A hundred or more boats littered the water, providing a kaleidoscopic ever-shifting light show. Hers was a standout, drawing applause from those ashore every time they drifted close.

And somehow in that moment, she understood what she'd been doing as if everything suddenly, finally made sense. *Tārā,* the Mistress of Liberation, had been setting her up for a long time without her being aware of it.

Like breaking through a bank of fog, the course she'd been sailing was so clear now that she could see it.

First, her entire library had gone digital, *except* for the tales of the great explorers and circumnavigators.

Then, she'd collected travel guides simply for the fun of imagining what was out there.

Third, *Tārā's* gear and sail-set were utterly ridiculous for kicking around Puget Sound—but perfect for heading off deep sea.

Even her job, she'd shifted to online and lately focused strictly on contract piecework. Log in, get it done, get paid, and move on.

It would have been nice to have someone to voyage with. Some part of her had kept her plans on hold, out of her own sight, but to no avail. In three years of waiting, she hadn't found the right fit once. Someone both serious and funny— the first to put up with her and the latter to lighten her up a little. She'd certainly heard that diagnosis from enough exes to believe it necessary. They had to be smart, independent, adventurous...

Yeah, her cat was, sadly, as close as she'd ever come.

Officially sick of waiting, only one question remained.

When?

Spring. Once the winter storms had abated, she'd head out. March, April at the latest.

And that's why she'd ultra-decorated this Christmas. She, *Tārā,* and Master Howl were saying goodbye to Seattle with far more style and flair than she usually managed in her day-to-day life.

She looked down at Master Howl.

"If we're off to conquer the high seas, I should have worn my pirate outfit."

10

———

"Your *what?*" Howie hadn't meant to shout. He suddenly had the undivided attention of every sailor within a dozen boat-lengths, as well the party currently rocking out on the Ivar's Restaurant barge.

Janine had gone quiet for the last twenty minutes or so, leaving it up to him to slowly adapt to navigating an unfamiliar boat through such heavy traffic. His nerves had finally pushed him to the far quieter northeast corner of Lake Union near Ivar's.

The Number 12 red marker buoy below the I-5 overpass bridge was a common turning point for summertime Duck Dodge races and he knew it well. He'd been using that to practice various turns as he learned more of how the boat handled under power. It would be very different under sail and he'd love to learn that too.

The parts of his mind that weren't occupied with learning were busy debating the best way to ask Janine if she needed a regular crew. Maybe she'd let him try the helm under sail.

And then she'd spoken—to herself and her cat—but

with the engine barely above an idle her voice had carried clearly.

"Your..." he tried to catch his breath. There was no way. She was several inches shorter than the woman who'd been stuck in his mind for the two weeks since he'd played the Pirate Santa. He'd considered breaking his rule and joining the yacht club simply to find her.

"My what?" She looked up at him. There were enough work lights in the nearby boatyard that he had his first really clear look at her face.

"Your...pirate outfit?" It was to be her.

She looked away—exactly as she had when he'd beckoned her to take her bow on the tabletop. "It's silly."

That's when he remembered her stepping so lightly on the chair to climb up on the table beside him. Her leather pirate boots had several inches of stout heel. It was her.

He considered not saying anything. *Oh, hi. I crashed your yacht-club party once, acting like a total lunatic. By the way, I think I may love you.*

Not a good start.

I've had this huge fantasy crush on you since...

Please let me bow at your feet, my pirate elf.

Yeah, a fast track course for a cold swim to shore.

And she thought that *she* was the one who'd been silly?

"Tell me," he eased the boat to port to avoid ramming a Christmas canoe that had twinkle lights twisted around the paddles. They even wore black outfits so that only the paddles showed. "I'll bet I can out-foolish you."

She shook her head and kept her silence.

"C'mon," he knew he was pleading, "how am I supposed to talk you into teaching me how to really sail if you won't tell me the embarrassing shit?"

She turned to face him, studying him in that quiet way he couldn't believe he hadn't recognized earlier.

"Okay. This is going to sound beyond stupid."

"I can out-do it. I swear on Master Howl's food bowl." That earned him a brief smile.

"I was recently in charge of a Pirate Christmas party. And there was this guy." Again one of those vast silences that shouted so loudly about who she was.

"I hate him already."

"He crashed the party as, you're not going to believe this, a Pirate Santa. He was loud, ridiculous—"

And curling up to die at the helm of your boat.

"—and probably the most decent guy I've met in years."

11

———

Howie had gone strangely quiet until they'd returned down through the Ballard Locks and had retied the boat at Shilshole. The only thing she could figure out was he must now deem her to be a total idiot. Who ever would get a crush on a Pirate Santa whose face she'd never seen.

His silence had let her dredge up thoughts she hadn't found in the last two weeks since the events of that night. And she let them out, tales told into the chill night.

The way he treated those kids.

With simple gifts, he gave those girls lofty visions of what they could be.

Without her realizing it, he'd sailed into her thoughts as smoothly as *Tārā* slicing through a wave. He'd been too loud and brash for her, and his Brooklyn accent had often grown almost incomprehensibly thick to her Iowan ear. But he'd... well, she'd liked him.

And the idea of finally heading out to cross the seas was so big and fresh that it too had spilled out of her. The fantasy of sailing from one exotic place to another, seeing the world. Making some money when she hit a port and could connect in; she owned her own floating home, so the costs were low and she could carry on for...years.

And why she'd dumped all of that on Howie still mystified her. He'd been quiet and listened. Somehow he made it okay for her to speak the thoughts she never said to anyone, not even Master Howl. Or herself.

It was only as they were tying off the spring line on the boat and plugging in the shore-power cable that she realized something. He'd convinced her to give him sailing lessons next weekend. And even made a tentative date for New Year's Eve if they went well.

But... "Hey, you never told me how you could *out-foolish* me."

Howie stood in the darkness beside her on the dock. The temperature had dropped enough that their breath issued as white clouds. By that alone, she could see that he'd tipped his head back to stare up at the stars.

They were crystal bright, at least for being so close to the parking lot and the low wash lights that lit the dock's planking. From deep sea? A thousand miles from the next nearest light? Janine couldn't wait to see them.

"Well, I'm not sure how to say this."

"Try." She'd laid out every ridiculous dream she had and needed someone, anyone, to tell her it wasn't a pile of steaming hooey, even this near stranger.

Howie leaned back against the hull of her boat, which drifted away from the dock, almost enough to plop his butt down into the water before the lines snubbed it to a halt. Once he stood squarely on the dock again, he let out a big cloud of breath, then turned to face her.

"Your dream is beyond beautiful, Janine. I can't find a way of saying how much I want to do it with you without sounding like a total stalker."

And he saw he was right as Janine shifted a step back along the dock.

Howie reached out a hand to stop her, but withdrew it before he touched her. He *so* wanted to touch her.

"Except maybe this…"

"What?" she asked when he didn't continue.

He took hope from how she'd described him and dug deep for his best Brooklyn-Jew-pirate, and spoke softly…

"Arrrr! The lovely Pirate Queen needs a Pirate Santa in her life, don't she?"

If you enjoyed this collection
please consider leaving a review.
They really help.

Want to join M. L.'s Readers Club?
https://rc.mlbuchman.com/join

Keep reading for an exciting excerpt from:
Where Dreams #1: *Where Dreams are Born*

WHERE DREAMS ARE BORN (EXCERPT)

IF YOU ENJOYED THAT, YOU'LL LOVE THIS TALE!

WHERE DREAMS ARE BORN
(EXCERPT)

Russell leaned his back against the studio door after he locked it behind the last of the staff. He barely managed the energy to turn off his camera.

He knew it was good. The images were there; he'd really captured them.

But something was missing.

The groove ran so clean when he slid into it. First his Manhattan high-ceilinged loft would fade into the background, then the strobe lights, reflector umbrellas, and green-screen backdrops all became texture and tone.

Image, camera, and man then became one and nothing else mattered—a single flow of light, beginning before time was counted, and ending its journey in the printed image. One ray of primordial light traveling forever to glisten off the BMW roadster still parked in one corner of the rough-planked wood floor worn smooth by generations of use. Another ray lost in the dark blackness of the finest leather bucket seats. A hundred more picking out the supermodel's perfect hand dangling a single shining and golden key—the image shot just slow enough that the key blurred as it spun, but the logo remained clear.

He couldn't quite put his finger on it...

It would be another great ad by Russell Morgan, Inc. The client would be knocked dead—the ad leaving all others standing still as it roared down the passing lane. This one might get him another Clio, or even a second Mobius.

But...

There wasn't usually a "but."

And there definitely wasn't supposed to be one.

The groove had definitely been there, but he hadn't been in it.

That was the problem. It had slid along, sweeping his staff into their own orchestrated perfection, but he'd remained untouched. That ideal, seamless flow hadn't included him at all.

"Be honest, boyo, that session sucked," he told the empty studio. Everything had come together so perfectly for yet another ad for yet another high-end glossy. *Man, the Magazine* would launch spectacularly in a few weeks, a high-profile mid-December launch, and it would include a never before seen twelve-page spread by the great Russell Morgan. The rag would probably never pay off the lavish launch party of hope, ice sculptures, and chilled magnums of champagne before disappearing like a thousand before it.

"Morose much?"

The studio kept its thoughts to itself—the first reliable sign that he wasn't totally losing his shit.

He stowed the last camera with the others piled by his computer. At the breaker box he shut off the umbrellas, spots, scoops, and washes. The studio shifted from a stark landscape in hard-edged relief to a nest of curious shadows and rounded forms. The tang of hot metal and deodorant were the only lasting result of the day's efforts.

"Get your shit together, Russell." His reflection in the darkened window, stories above the streetlights of West 10th, was unimpressed and proved it was wise enough to not answer back. There was never a "down" after a shoot; there was always an "up."

Not tonight.

He'd kept everyone late—even though it was Thanksgiving eve—hoping for that smooth slide of image-camera-man. It was only when he saw the power of the images he captured that he knew he wasn't a part of the chain anymore and decided he'd paid enough triple-time expenses.

The next to last two-page spread would be the killer—shot with the door open against a background as black as the sports car's finish, the model's single perfect leg wrapped in thigh-high red-leather boots all that was visible in the driver's seat. The sensual juxtaposition of woman and sleek machine served as an irresistible focus. It was an ad designed to wrap every person with even a hint of a Y-chromosome around its little finger. And those with only X-chromosomes would simply want to be her. He'd shot a perfect combo of sex for the guys and power for the women.

Even the final one-page image, a close-up of driver's seat from exactly the same angle, revealing not the model but instead a single rose of precisely the same hue as the leather boot, hadn't moved him despite its perfection.

Without him noticing, Russell had become no more than the observer, merely a technician behind the camera. Now that he faced it, months, maybe even a year had passed since he'd been yanked all the way into the light-image-camera-man slipstream. Tonight was a wakeup call and he didn't like it one bit. Wakeup calls happened to others, not him. But tonight he could no longer ignore it, he hadn't even trailed along in the churned-up wake.

"You're just a creative cog in the advertising machine." Ouch! That one stung, but it didn't turn aside the relentless steamroller of his thoughts speeding down some empty, godforsaken autobahn.

His career was roaring ahead, his business' growth running fast and smooth. But, now that he considered it, he really didn't give a damn.

His life looked perfect, but—"Don't think it!"—his autobahn mind finished despite the command, *it wasn't.*

Russell left his silent reflection to its own thoughts and went through the back door that led to his apartment— closing it tightly on the perfect BMW, the perfect rose, and somewhere, lost among a hundred other props from dozens of other shoots, the long pair of perfect red-leather Chanel boots that had been wrapped around the most expensive legs in Manhattan. He didn't care if he never walked back through that door again. He'd been doing his art by rote; how god-awful sad was that?

And just to rub salt in the wound, he shot *commercial* art.

He'd never had the patience to do art for art's sake. Delayed gratification was his idea of no fun at all. He left the apartment dark with only the city's soft glow through the blind-covered windows revealing the vaguest outlines of the framed art on the wall. Even that almost overwhelmed him tonight.

He didn't want to see the huge prints by the *art* artists: autographed Goldsworthy, Liebowitz, and Joseph Francis' photomosaics for the moderns. A hundred and fifty rare, even one-of-a-kind prints adorned his walls—all the way back through Bourke-White to Russell's prize, an original

Daguerre. The Museum of Modern Art kept begging to borrow his collection for a show...and at the moment he was half tempted to dump the whole lot in their Dumpster if they didn't want it.

Crossing the one-room loft apartment—as spacious as the studio—he bypassed the circle of avant-garde chairs that were almost as uncomfortable as they looked and avoided the lush black-leather wrap-around sectional sofa of such ludicrous scale that it could be a playpen for two or host a party for twenty. He cracked the fridge in the stainless-steel-and-black corner kitchen searching for something other than his usual beer.

A bottle of Krug.

Maybe he was just being grouchy after a long day's work.

Juice.

No. He'd run his enthusiasm into the ground but good.

Milk even.

Would he miss the camera if he never picked it up again?

No reaction.

Nothing.

Not even an itch in his palm.

That was an emptiness he did not want to face. Especially not alone, in his apartment, in the middle of the world's most vibrant city.

Russell turned away, and just as the door swung closed, the last sliver of light—the relentless chilly blue-white of the refrigerator bulb—shone across his bed. A quick grab snagged the edge of the door and left the narrow beam illuminating a long pale form on his black-silk bedspread.

The Chanel boots weren't in the studio after all. They were still wrapped around those three thousand dollar-an-hour legs: the only clothing on a perfect body. Five foot-eleven of intensely toned female anatomy right down to an exquisitely stair-mastered behind. Her long, white-blonde hair lay as a perfect Godiva over her tanned breasts—except for their too exact symmetry, even the closest inspection didn't reveal the work done there. She lay with one leg raised just ever so slightly to hide what was meant to be revealed later.

Melanie.

By the steady rise and fall of her flat stomach, he knew she'd fallen asleep while waiting for him to finish in the studio.

How long had they been an item? Two months? Three?

She'd made him feel alive…at least when he was actually with her. Melanie was the super-model in his bed or on his arm at yet another SoHo gallery opening. Together they journeyed to sharp parties and trendy three-star restaurants where she dazzled and wooed yet another gathering of New York's finest with her ever so soft, so sensual, and so studied French accent. Together they were wired into the heart of the in-crowd.

But that wasn't him, was it? It didn't sound like the Russell he once knew.

Perhaps "they" were about how *he* looked on *her* arm?

Did she know tomorrow was the annual Thanksgiving ordeal at his parents? The grand holiday gathering that he'd rather die than attend? Any number of eligible woman would be floating about his parents' house out in Greenwich; anyone able to finagle an invitation would attend in hopes of snaring one of *People Magazine's* "100 Most Eligible." They all wanted to land the heir to a billion or some such; though he was wealthy enough on his own, by his own sweat, to draw anyone's attention. He ranked number twenty-four on the list this year—up from forty-seven the year before despite Tom Cruise being available yet again.

But not Melanie. He knew that it wasn't the money that drew her. Yes, she wanted him. But even more, she wanted the life that came with him—wrapped in the man-package. She wanted The Life. The one that *People Magazine* readers dreamed about between glossy pages.

His fingertips were growing cold where they held the refrigerator door cracked open.

If he woke her there'd be amazing sex. Or a great party to go to. Or...

Did he want "Or"? What more did he want from her?

Sex. Companionship. An energy, a vivacity, a thirst he feared that he lacked. Yes.

But where was that smooth synchronicity hiding, like the light-image-camera-man of photography that he'd lost? Where lurked that perfect flow from one person to another? Did she feel it? Could he ever feel it? Did it even exist?

"More?" he whispered into the darkness to test the sound. He knew all about wanting more.

The refrigerator door slid shut—escaping from his numbed fingers—which plunged the apartment back into darkness, taking Melanie along with it.

His breath echoed in the vast darkness. Proof that he was alive if nothing more.

It was time to close the studio—time to be done with Russell Incorporated.

Then what?

Maybe Angelo would know what to do. He always claimed that he did. Maybe this time Russell would actually listen to his almost-brother, though he knew from the experience of being himself for the last thirty years that was unlikely.

Seattle.

Damn! He'd have to go to bloody Seattle to find his best friend. There was a possible upside to such a trip—maybe there'd be a flight out before tomorrow's mess at his parents'. He slapped his pocket, but once again he'd set his phone down in some unknown corner of the studio and it would take forever to find. He really needed two—one chained down so that he could always find it to call the other.

Russell considered the darkness. He could guarantee that Seattle wouldn't be a big hit with Melanie.

Now if he only knew whether that was a good thing or bad.

———

Keep reading now!
A great tale of romance and adventure,
Of sailboats, food, fashion, and fun.
Available at fine retailers everywhere.
Where Dreams are Born

And please don't forget that review for
The Complete Sailing Stories.

ABOUT THE AUTHOR

USA Today and Amazon #1 Bestseller M. L. "Matt" Buchman has 70+ action-adventure thriller and military romance novels, 125 short stories, and lotsa audiobooks. PW says: "Tom Clancy fans open to a strong female lead will clamor for more." Booklist declared: "3X Top 10 of the Year." He is also the editor of the quarterly anthology magazine *Thrill Ride.*

A project manager with a geophysics degree, he's designed and built houses, flown and jumped out of planes, solo-sailed a 50' sailboat, and bicycled solo around the world...and he quilts. More at: www.mlbuchman.com.

Other works by M. L. Buchman: *(* - also in audio)*

Action-Adventure Thrillers

Dead Chef
One Chef!
Two Chef!

Miranda Chase
*Drone**
*Thunderbolt**
*Condor**
*Ghostrider**
*Raider**
*Chinook**
*Havoc**
*White Top**
*Start the Chase**
*Lightning**
*Skibird**
*Nightwatch**

Science Fiction / Fantasy

Deities Anonymous
Cookbook from Hell: Reheated
Saviors 101

Contemporary Romance

Eagle Cove
Return to Eagle Cove
Recipe for Eagle Cove
Longing for Eagle Cove
Keepsake for Eagle Cove

Love Abroad
Heart of the Cotswolds: England
Path of Love: Cinque Terre, Italy

Where Dreams
Where Dreams are Born
Where Dreams Reside
*Where Dreams Are of Christmas**
Where Dreams Unfold
Where Dreams Are Written
Where Dreams Continue

Non-Fiction

Strategies for Success
Managing Your Inner Artist/Writer
*Estate Planning for Authors**
Character Voice
*Narrate and Record Your Own Audiobook**

Short Story Series by M. L. Buchman:

Action-Adventure Thrillers

Dead Chef

Miranda Chase Origin Stories

Romantic Suspense

Antarctic Ice Fliers

US Coast Guard

Contemporary Romance

Eagle Cove

Other

Deities Anonymous (fantasy)

Single Titles

The Emily Beale Universe
(military romantic suspense)

The Night Stalkers
MAIN FLIGHT
The Night Is Mine
I Own the Dawn
Wait Until Dark
Take Over at Midnight
Light Up the Night
Bring On the Dusk
By Break of Day
Target of the Heart
Target Lock on Love
Target of Mine
Target of One's Own
Night Stalkers Holidays
*Daniel's Christmas**
*Frank's Independence Day**
*Peter's Christmas**
Christmas at Steel Beach
*Zachary's Christmas**
*Roy's Independence Day**
*Damien's Christmas**
Christmas at Peleliu Cove

Henderson's Ranch
*Nathan's Big Sky**
*Big Sky, Loyal Heart**
*Big Sky Dog Whisperer**
*Tales of Henderson's Ranch**

Shadow Force: Psi
*At the Slightest Sound**
*At the Quietest Word**
*At the Merest Glance**
*At the Clearest Sensation**

White House Protection Force
*Off the Leash**
*On Your Mark**
*In the Weeds**

Firehawks
Pure Heat
Full Blaze
*Hot Point**
*Flash of Fire**
Wild Fire
Smokejumpers
*Wildfire at Dawn**
*Wildfire at Larch Creek**
*Wildfire on the Skagit**

Delta Force
*Target Engaged**
*Heart Strike**
*Wild Justice**
*Midnight Trust**

Emily Beale Universe Short Story Series
The Night Stalkers
The Night Stalkers Stories
The Night Stalkers CSAR
The Night Stalkers Wedding Stories
The Future Night Stalkers

Delta Force
Th Delta Force Shooters
The Delta Force Warriors

Firehawks
The Firehawks Lookouts
The Firehawks Hotshots
The Firebirds

White House Protection Force
Stories

Future Night Stalkers
Stories (Science Fiction)

SIGN UP FOR M. L. BUCHMAN'S NEWSLETTER TODAY

and receive:
Release News
Free Short Stories
a Free Book

Get your free book today. Do it now.
free-book.mlbuchman.com

Or join his Reader's Club:
https://rc.mlbuchman.com/join

www.ingramcontent.com/pod-product-compliance
Lightning Source LLC
Chambersburg PA
CBHW050150120726
47903CB00002B/563